MR. LINCOLN'S
DRUMMER

MR. LINCOLN'S DRUMMER

G. Clifton Wisler

SCHOLASTIC INC.
New York Toronto London Auckland Sydney

ISBN 0-590-86525-0

12 11 10 9 8 7 6 5 4 3 2 1   7 8 9/9 0 1 2/0

Printed in the U.S.A.   40
First Scholastic printing, February 1997

*This book is
reverently dedicated
to all the boys, in all the wars,
who never came back.*

Roll of the Third Vermont Volunteer Infantry Regiment in the Union Army of the Potomac, 1861–62

ARMY COMMANDER:
Maj. Gen. George B. McClellan

SIXTH CORPS COMMANDER:
Brig. Gen. William B. Franklin

SECOND DIVISION COMMANDER:
Brig. Gen. William F. "Baldy" Smith

SECOND (VERMONT) BRIGADE COMMANDER:
Brig. Gen. W. T. H. Brooks

Third Vermont Infantry Regiment, 1861–62

REGIMENTAL COMMANDER: Col. Breed Hyde
(Union regiments originally contained ten companies of
approximately 100 men each.)

COMPANY D

COMPANY COMMANDER: Capt. Fernando C. Harrington

First Lt. David G. Kenesson

Second Lt. Erastus Buck

Sgt. William M. Currier

various privates

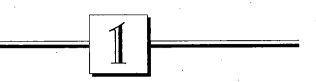

A DRUM IS THE HEARTBEAT of an army. Its tempo lets you know whether to hurry along, steady yourself, or take to your heels. It tells you when to get up, eat, and go to bed. And the fellow who taps out the calls is the very heart of every company in every regiment in every army.

They called us drummer boys.

For my part, I came to the war sort of by accident. In April of '61, when the Carolina rebels fired on the flag at Fort Sumter down in Charleston, I was just ten years old. Except for some bold talk by a few older boys and three long-winded speeches by an abolitionist preacher who had come up from Boston, nobody in town paid much attention to the news that we were at war with the South. It wasn't that we Vermonters weren't patriotic. We had crops to tend and business of our own to mind, though. At least that's what Pa told me.

Everything changed the first week of June.

"Come look at the soldiers, Willie!" my little brother Charley had shouted to me from the street. "There's thousands of them!"

There weren't, of course, but I didn't know that until I had raced out the door and seen for myself. Truth be told, there were no more than a handful of real soldiers.

The rest were tall, skinny farm boys from the neighboring counties. I spied one or two I knew, and I waved to them.

"We've answered Mr. Lincoln's call!" Cal Stebbins, a boy from up the road, called to me.

"You're not old enough to soldier, Cal!" I hollered.

"I'm eighteen," he yelled back. "And we're taking some even younger."

"How young?" I shouted.

"Not as young as you, Willie Johnston!" Ma cried, grabbing me by the ear. "Don't you have work waiting?"

"Yes, ma'am," I confessed as she unclamped my ear. "I just thought I'd have a look."

"Sure," she said, gazing skeptically at me with her tired blue eyes. "That's all you're ever about, looking and asking and idling like some stray pup run off from a farm. You're a working boy, or have you forgotten that again?"

"I haven't," I insisted. "I'm not yet apprenticed, though, Ma, and it isn't every day soldiers march down Main Street. In Saint Johnsbury, at least."

"Thank the Lord for that," she grumbled. "It's hard enough to keep youngsters at their labors without such foolish distractions."

"I thought you favored freeing the slaves, Ma," I said, putting on my serious face. "Just last Sunday—"

"Don't start up now, William J. Johnston," she warned. "You'll not escape the cutting table so easily."

I shook my head and sighed. There was no use arguing with Ma when she went to using my whole name like that. I sneaked a final peek at Cal and the rest of the recruits. Then I stumbled back to the shop and slithered through the door.

"Now, to work," Ma said, pointing to the bolts of fabric stacked on the long wooden table to my left. My older brother James sat on the far side of my empty chair, frowning. He was closing in on fourteen, but I used to think that he was born old.

"Somebody has to be serious around here," he told me once. "You manage enough mischief for ten families, Willie."

Once Ma left us to our work, James set aside his shears and stared at the door.

"Are there very many of them?" he asked.

"Not so many," I replied. "Cal Stebbins is with them. A few boys we know from the farms upriver. A fair number from Brighton."

"It sure seems exciting, joining Mr. Lincoln's army and marching south to thrash those rebels!" James confessed. "It's sure to be over before I'm old enough to go."

"Cal said they're taking some young ones," I whispered.

"Oh, I heard about that, Willie, but to go, you have to get your parents to sign something."

"Pa might," I suggested.

"Ma wouldn't," he insisted. "Besides, who would keep the shop going? Who would look after Ma and Charley?"

"That's Pa's job," I argued.

"Sure it is," James agreed. "But when has he ever done it?"

I wanted to argue, but it was impossible to talk James around to your point of view. He never said much, and even then, it was after he sat there, scratching his ear and chewing on the words for a while.

"Pa dreams," I muttered.

3

"He dreams too much," James grumbled.

I suppose it was a fault Pa and I shared. Ma thought so anyway.

"Dreaming won't get those pages read," she scolded whenever I set down my schoolbooks and stared off out the window. "Dreams don't pay our debts," she would tell Pa.

Sure, Pa had his faults. But after all, he hadn't been much older than James when he had signed onto a ship sailing from Bristol to Boston.

"The future's America," he had told his family. "Any English lad with gumption is bound to go there."

Whatever else you said about Pa, you had to admit that he had gumption. He had taught himself to read and write, learned a half dozen trades, and worked his way west to New York by the time I was born. He was running a small shop in Morristown, and Ma told me once that we were doing pretty well there. Then Pa got the itch to move on, and we headed east into the Green Mountains of Vermont. By 1860 we were settled in Saint Johnsbury, or Saint Jay as some called it for short. Pa bought a two-story house in town, and he operated a tailor shop downstairs. He and Ma shared a room at the top of the stairs, and we three boys crowded into a smaller chamber next door, which was intended to be an attic.

Saint Jay wasn't Boston, and trade was never all that plentiful. Pa got most of his business altering trousers to fit younger brothers or patching knees and elbows worn out of Sunday suits. Ma did most of the real work, making shirts and dresses of cheap gingham cloth bought off one of the mills down on the Connecticut River. As soon as James and I were old enough, she set us to help-

4

ing trace patterns and cut cloth when we got home from school. Even Charley, who was barely five, cut scraps into quilting squares. The Keller sisters, a pair of widows, fashioned them into coverlets for the Caledonia County Orphans Home.

I never suspected it that afternoon, but the war brought us more business than I would have imagined. The next day, when James and I clambered downstairs to have our breakfast, a tall, bewhiskered fellow in a fine wool suit stood talking with Pa just inside the door.

"James, Willie," Pa said, waving us to his side. "Shake hands with Colonel Hyde, the new commander of the Third Vermont Volunteers."

James offered his hand, and the colonel shook it. I just stared at the man. The Hydes were about as famous a family as there was in the state. The colonel's grandfather had fought at Bunker Hill with the patriots, and his father was a hero of the War of 1812. I'd read in the newspaper Mrs. Perkins tacked to the wall at school how Mr. Breed Hyde had been called to lead the new regiment to war.

"How are you, young man?" the colonel asked.

"Just fine, Colonel," I replied, gazing down at my toes. "I guess you'll be marching south to punish those rebels any day now."

"I judge it will not be long," the colonel said, clasping my hand. "I hope we have time to train the men. They are pitifully short of discipline. At any rate, you will have the uniforms ready next week, won't you, Mr. Johnston?"

"If we have to sew all night," Pa promised.

"And the price is agreeable?" Colonel Hyde asked.

"Generous," Pa replied. "I wish I could make a gift of them, but . . ."

"Nonsense," the colonel said, laughing. "What would the world come to if an honest Yankee tailor could not make a profit? Is that not why we are fighting?"

"I thought we were fighting to free the slaves," I said, wrinkling my forehead.

Ma gave me a hush sign, and Pa scowled. James grabbed my hand and led me to the table.

"No, the boy's right," Colonel Hyde added. "We fight to preserve the Union and to guarantee all Americans the freedom our forefathers died to win. It is important for every soldier to understand his purpose and his duty. We are certain to achieve victory because our cause is just. Our men will see it clearly. It is our great advantage over the rebels."

That next week the soldiers enjoyed a considerably greater amount of freedom than any of us Johnstons did. Colonel Hyde was just one of the officers to visit Pa's shop, and we had nearly twenty uniforms to cut and sew. Pa traveled to Concord to get boxes of brass buttons with an angry-looking eagle on the front. A freighter brought us three bolts of fine wool cloth, and I helped James dye the individual pieces in a vat of putrid stain that turned the garments a bold shade of gray.

The color they chose brought the regiment some problems later, but at the time the Thirders, as folks in Saint Jay called them, looked neat and warlike in their gray trousers and tunics. They camped just outside town on the grounds of the Caledonia County Agriculture Society, which someone had renamed Camp Baxter in honor of some general or other. Each day I delivered a uniform or two to the officers, or to a soldier with the means to pay for better clothes. Often I'd stay and visit with Cal Stebbins and the three Stevens brothers from Brighton, all soldiering in the same company. Other times I would wander off and watch whatever batch was marching up and down, drilling.

"You the tailor's boy?" a slight-shouldered boy of about fifteen asked me one afternoon.

"Willie Johnston," I said, offering him my hand.

"Julian Scott," he replied as he took my hand and gave it a squeeze. "Company E fifer."

The fife was stuck in his trousers pocket. He had a sketch pad and two charcoals in his free hand.

"Mind if I have a look?" I asked, nodding to his drawings.

"Go ahead," he said, shyly passing me the sketch pad. "I'm not any too accomplished just yet, but I'm improving."

"They're good," I argued as I examined the drawings. "It's a fine likeness of the camp. I even recognize a few of the faces."

"It's hard to find time between drill and fife practice. Some of the real soldiers run into town now and then, but the lieutenant keeps me busy copying out his reports. Nobody can read anything he scribbles."

"Life's not a lot better for a tailor's son," I told him. "School's finished for the summer, but Pa just adds new chores to the old ones."

"I see you out here bringing uniforms," Julian said, taking a quick glance behind him. "You help your pa much with the sewing?"

"Ma does most of that," I explained. "I sew on buttons. That's pretty easy. Lately I've been putting some of the cuffs on, too."

"Ever made a pair of trousers fit?" he asked.

I grinned as he opened up his tunic and showed me his waist. His trousers must have been half again as wide as needed. Julian was only two or three inches over five feet tall, and I guess he weighed ninety pounds.

"Vermonters as a rule run tall," he explained. "I don't think they expected they'd need to outfit a half-grown fifer."

"I can sew it up," I told him. "But you really ought to come to the house and let Ma do it. That way you won't have so much uniform sticking out from behind."

"I make too much of a target this way, don't I?" he asked, laughing.

"Oh, I figure the rebs will be running. They won't have time to shoot anybody," I declared.

"Don't you go counting on that," Julian warned. "I know the papers say it will be a short war, but I listen to the officers talking. They know those Southern generals. I'd say we'll have a fight of it. You'll likely be a soldier yourself before it's all over."

"I don't turn eleven until July," I grumbled.

"Then maybe you'll miss it after all. Me, I might have waited, but there's nothing I haven't sketched in the mountains."

"Sure," I said, nodding. "Not much happening hereabouts. We even have a stream here called the Sleepers River."

"I don't plan to sleep through this war," Julian boasted. "No, I want to be right in the middle of it."

"Then you can't wear those pants," I insisted. "Tell your lieutenant you've got to go into town. We'll get Ma to fix 'em for you."

Julian picked up a pass, and we walked back into Saint Jay together. Ma had three uniforms to finish, and she wasn't all that eager to take on more work, especially when I whispered that Julian wasn't long on money. When she got a look at him, though, she melted like butter on a hot roll.

"Men," she muttered. "Sending boys into battle. It's a crime! Come over here and let me have a look. Well, there's no arguing. Let me mark those pants and cut them down for you."

"Thanks, ma'am," Julian said. "If you could just stitch 'em some, I'd be grateful. I only have half a dollar . . ."

"Nonsense," she scolded. "I wouldn't send Willie out in such an outfit, and he'll tell you himself he's not earned too much consideration lately, loafing as he does."

Ma stood the little fifer up next to a long mirror and marked his trousers with chalk. Then he skinned out of his pants, and she started altering them.

"Leave 'em big enough to allow for some growing," Julian urged.

"Growing?" Ma asked, gazing at one of his skinny legs. "I don't believe they feed you soldiers enough to allow for growing. Willie, run to the kitchen and find some cookies. This child gets any thinner, his pants will slide right off him, altered or not."

Julian started to argue, but I motioned him to hush. In half a minute I was back with lemonade and the cookies. The way he ate, you would have suspected Ma was right about the army and its feeding habits. I'm no small eater myself, but I never once saw anybody gobble so many cookies in such a short time. Julian was gnawing a loaf of bread when Ma finished the trousers. He slipped them on, grinned, and thanked us both.

"It seems little enough," Ma replied, dabbing her eyes

with a cloth. "My James is your age. I hope he doesn't have to join the army any time soon."

"May be over before long," Julian told her. "Thanks again, Mrs. Johnston. You stop by and visit Company E next time you get out to Camp Baxter, Willie."

"I'll do that," I promised.

Julian left then, and I headed for the cutting table. We each had our jobs to do, and I knew Ma was waiting to make sure mine got done. Colonel Hyde could look after Julian.

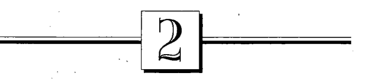

THE THIRD VERMONT remained at Camp Baxter until
July 24. I was out there every few days myself, deliv-
ering uniforms or picking up trousers that required
mending. I could nearly always stretch each visit without
landing myself in too much hot water. Ma got used to
my lateness. Generally she just nodded and pointed to
the cutting table.

"They still drilling?" James sometimes asked.

"Mostly," I whispered. "They're shooting some now.
Just targets, though. No rebs handy."

When there wasn't too much work waiting for me at
the shop, I would sit around with Cal Stebbins, swapping opinions on the war.

"You afraid, Cal?" I asked him one day when we were
alone.

"Afraid?" he asked, stomping his foot down hard on
the rocky ground. "Only thing I'm scared of is that the
fellows already down there will chase the rebs home before the Third gets its chance to fight!"

Julian wasn't half so boastful.

"I listen to the officers, and I look over the regiment,"
he told me that same afternoon. "Between measles and
idlers, I don't count us more than five hundred strong.
A regiment ought to muster in at a thousand men."

It was Julian who taught me the drum calls. Company E's drummer was one of the boys down with measles, and his drum just lay there gathering dust. Julian handed it over, found the sticks, and had me tapping out each call.

"You pick it up real fast," he told me. "You're near as good as most of our drummers right now."

"Ma's got an ear for music," I explained. "She sings in the church choir, and she's always encouraged us boys. My brother James plays a fiddle."

"Well, if you ever get tired of patching trousers, you go and talk with the colonel. Armies can always use a spare musician or two."

For just a second I considered it, but I knew Ma would march into camp and drag me home like a wayward pup. There I was, eleven years old now and creeping up on five feet tall. To her, though, I was still a half-pint.

Word of the big battle at Bull Run reached Saint Johnsbury the day before the Third left town. The rebs had turned back General McDowell's loyal regiments at a little stream in northern Virginia. It had started out like a Sunday social, with congressmen, senators, and fine ladies all sitting on a hill to watch the sport. By the time it was over, those folks were scrambling back to Washington on foot, and the Union army was shaken, shattered, and thoroughly disheartened. A fair number on both sides had been shot, and hundreds of Mr. Lincoln's soldiers were now captive.

"We're headed south, to Baltimore," Julian told me that next morning. He had come to the shop to give Ma a pair of drawings as payment for her work on his trousers.

"You watch out for those rebs," I warned.

12

"Let the men lead the charges," Ma urged. "You hold back, Julian. Grow older."

"Musicians have to spur the men onward," Julian said, puffing himself up as tall as possible. "Don't worry, though. There's not all that much of me to shoot at."

I cracked a smile, but Ma frowned. She was pure maple opposed to boys joining the army, and Julian standing there in his neat gray tunic and trousers reminded her that James and I weren't much younger.

The whole town gathered near the depot and watched the Third march to the waiting rail cars. Close to nine hundred soldiers formed neat lines and columns. A twenty-four–piece band led the way, and we cheered each company as it marched past us and boarded the train.

"Wave to them, Willie," Ma suggested as the locomotive blew its whistle.

I raised my hand, but I couldn't manage much enthusiasm. The windows were filled with gray caps and dour faces, but you couldn't make out anybody in particular. There were too many wives and mothers and brothers and sisters between us and the train.

"It's a sad thing, leaving your home," Pa observed that night as we sat down at the dinner table. "I wish those boys well. A part of me goes with them."

I knew he was remembering the day he said good-bye to his family and set sail for America. He never spoke much about that, but his eyes betrayed his sadness.

"Just children, most of them," Ma grumbled. "Too young to fight a war."

"They're doing what they consider best," James argued. "I know three or four of them. They judge it better they should go than their fathers."

"Some fathers and sons both are going," I pointed out. "Jerry Bishop and his pa are serving with Cal Stebbins in Company D."

"Jerry's hardly seventeen," Ma objected. "What can Jeremiah be thinking?"

"There are boys even younger going to beat the drum or play the fife," I reminded her.

"I know," she said, bowing her head and holding her hands out to each side. "We'll pray for them tonight."

We had the habit of linking hands around the dinner table while Ma or Pa said a prayer, and we did it like always that night. There was a difference, though. Usually the prayer asked a blessing on the food, on our house, and on each of us Johnstons. That night Ma remembered the young soldiers, and we added our individual amens.

The Third's departure hit us particularly hard. Not just our hearts, either. With the soldiers gone, we were back to patching torn trousers and altering hand-me-downs. With so many men gone off to fight, lots of women tried to support themselves by sewing. Work became scarce. Ma found it hard to match the prices asked by some of the farm women, and on top of that, prices on everything from milk and flour to needles and thread soared. Pa had whole boxes of brass buttons and no uniforms to sew them onto. It took most of the uniform profits to pay our bills, and we were soon faced with difficult choices.

Ma and Pa didn't talk much about our troubles, but I read the wrinkles on their foreheads. That autumn I left school early every day so as to help. I picked up a nickel here and there by stocking shelves at the mercantile. Sometimes I'd hire myself out on one of the nearby farms. Nobody paid much for a skinny waif of eleven, but each time I dropped a few coins in Ma's purse, I felt a little taller.

News from the war was nearly as bad. The rebs had thrashed General Lyon's army in Missouri, killing the general himself at a place called Wilson's Creek and threatening to march on Saint Louis. There wasn't much fighting in the East, but from time to time the newspaper carried reports of a man from the Third who had died of sickness.

"Are things as bad as they're saying at school?" I asked Pa one night after dinner.

"I'm no expert, son," he replied, "but I judge an army doesn't do much good camped in the shadow of the capital. Sooner or later Mr. Lincoln has to order the boys back into Virginia, and there will be fighting and bleeding aplenty when he does."

The fighting and bleeding came later. By November, the Third was finding its ranks thinned by sickness and desertions. Some of the farm boys found they couldn't abide the discipline, and others simply got homesick. Every few days a pair of soldiers rode through town, looking for some fellow or another. Then, around the middle of the month, Captain Fernando Harrington arrived in Saint Jay.

"The Union's in peril!" he proclaimed. "We need men. Stay clear, you fainthearted fellows. We don't want you. The Third's a proud regiment, and she calls all true sons of Vermont to join the colors. As Ethan Allen and his brave Green Mountain lads stood tall against the British, we must stand now for the Union."

The captain made speeches every day, but he didn't get many men to sign the muster book. For one thing, he had no knack for drawing a crowd. Snow had begun to fall by then, and nearly everybody stayed indoors. Even when the sun did shine, most people were too busy to stop and listen to a soldier ramble on and on.

One afternoon I spied the captain sitting alone outside the courthouse. I was headed home after raking out Mr. Murdock's stable, and I couldn't help feeling sorry for Captain Harrington.

"You should talk to the ministers," I suggested. "Talk on Sunday, when you have a crowd there to listen."

"I plan to," the captain replied. "But I have to leave next week. So far I haven't filled my roster. I need eighteen more men."

"You have to let people know you're here," I insisted. "I saw recruiters down in Manchester. They had a drummer."

"I've got a drum, but I'm afraid our drummer missed his mother. He left en route."

The captain pointed toward the courthouse door. A drum rested there.

"I could beat assembly," I offered. "I remember that one."

"Remember?" he asked.

"I watched the men drill last summer," I explained. "Julian Scott, Company E's fifer, taught me the calls."

"Give it a try then, son."

"Name's Willie," I said, hopping over and taking the drum in hand. "Willie Johnston."

"I don't suppose you're eighteen?" he asked.

"Just eleven," I confessed. "Tall for eleven, though."

"Still eleven," he muttered. "You aren't an orphan by any chance?"

"Got a ma, pa, and two brothers," I told him as I

16

slung the drum sash over my shoulder and gripped the sticks. "Ready?"

He nodded, and I began beating assembly. He nudged my side and yelled, "Louder!"

I slowed my tempo and banged harder. Soon the noise filled the street. Shopkeepers and schoolboys trotted out to see what was happening. Farmers paused outside the feed and grain. The captain told me to stop, and I silenced the drum. The beat was still echoing through my ears when he stood up on a stool and began speaking once again.

Captain Harrington was a smallish fellow, no more than five foot nine in his boots. His black hair was oiled and combed flat, and a small trim mustache curled up from his lip. When he spoke, his eyes caught fire, and from time to time he drew out his sword and waved it in the air.

I didn't pay much attention to his words, but others did. Three farm boys stepped forward and signed up then and there. One older man asked about a bonus. The captain explained he had fifty dollars ready to hand each and every recruit upon swearing in.

"Can't have the money first?" the man asked.

"Josh Dinsmore, you come away from there," a woman shouted. "Fifty dollars indeed! You know you would only spend it on whiskey, and what use would the army have for you then?"

The crowd had a good laugh at Mr. Dinsmore, and Captain Harrington waved him away.

Once those who wished to sign up had done so, the captain explained when and where they were to assemble. He then asked me to beat the drum once again. We attracted a second, smaller crowd that time, but one more man signed up.

"You've done your country a service this day, Willie," Captain Harrington said afterward. "Perhaps I can count on you tomorrow as well?"

"I'll ask my folks," I replied. "I might have chores."

"Hire someone to do them," he urged, flipping me a silver dollar. "I'll have a second one waiting for you tomorrow."

"I have to ask," I told him, "but I don't imagine it should be much of a problem."

It wasn't, either. Ma accepted the nickel I'd earned from Mr. Murdock for cleaning his stable, patted my back, and waved me toward a washbasin.

"Scrub good," she urged. "It wouldn't do to mix stable straw and roast beef."

"Oh, I forgot about this," I said, grinning as I set the silver dollar on the table.

"Willie?" she cried. "Did you rob the bank?"

"No," I said, trying not to blurt out the news.

"Explain, young man."

"Captain Harrington, the recruiter for the Third Vermont, paid me to beat the drum," I told her. "If I come back and do it again tomorrow, he'll give me another dollar."

"Just for beating the drum?" she asked. "You don't even know how."

"Julian taught me," I explained. "Last summer. I'm not too good at some calls, but all the captain really wants is enough noise to draw a crowd. He signed up four men today."

"I don't know that I like this, Willie," she muttered. "Soldiers aren't the best company for a boy. The weather could turn, too."

"We need the money, though, don't we?" I asked.

18

She nodded sadly, and I squeezed her hand. "Then I'll go on beating the drum, and we'll have another dollar."

I earned three of them altogether. I might have gotten a fourth, but Pa stopped by on Friday, and he told the captain four dollars was more than the job deserved.

"I don't know that I agree," Captain Harrington argued. "The boy does a fine job with the drum. Before he came along, I wasn't enjoying much success."

"Three dollars is a small fortune these days for anybody," Pa insisted. "Mrs. Johnston's surely spent it or I would insist Willie return it. A man shouldn't accept pay for doing his nation such a minor service."

"A grateful nation should reward her citizens," Captain Harrington declared. "The army pays men to serve. Even so, we can't get enough to fill our ranks."

"It's hard to imagine," Pa said, gripping my shoulders with his tired hands. "You pay what, thirteen dollars a month? That's more than most of us earn, and you feed and clothe soldiers, too."

"We're paying a fifty dollar bounty now as well," the captain added.

"Well, you're certain to draw more men," Pa declared. "Likely some of them have to talk it over with their wives."

"Perhaps," the captain agreed.

I felt a little uneasy about the conversation, but Pa seemed in such a good mood when we walked home together that I set aside my concern. We swapped jokes, and he laughed more than he had in months. Then, that night after dinner, I heard him talking with Ma in a deep, somber voice.

"There's nothing else to do," he told her. "It's my duty."

So that was it. Pa had decided to join up. I know that it had troubled him for some time that others were fighting. The war was going poorly, too. Even so, he might have stayed out of the army if business had been better. Things being what they were, the thirteen dollars a private earned each month was a regular fortune.

"You can cope with what little work we're getting nowadays, Elizabeth," he told Ma. "It won't get better. The army's buying up all the wool, and with cotton shut off from the South, the mills are no longer spinning inexpensive cotton cloth. No one in Vermont has the means of ordering a new suit at the prices we have to charge."

"There are other jobs," Ma argued.

"They'll pay me an enlistment bonus, Elizabeth. I'll be able to send you most of my pay, and there will be one less mouth to feed."

"And what about the boys? They need a father's hand."

"I've never been half as good at keeping them out of trouble as you are," Pa objected. "James is old enough to help, and in truth, he's already a better tailor than his father. Willie can be a handful, but in a pinch, he'll do you proud."

"Will, I can't manage alone," Ma insisted.

"You can," Pa said, sighing. "You have been for most of the last few months. This war won't last forever. I'll come back, and we'll have money to build a better future."

Sunday morning we sat silently in church while Captain Harrington made another speech about joining the army. Pa had told us that morning at breakfast that he was joining, and we had silently nodded. I had already told James, and Charley had heard from him.

"I could go in your place," James had offered.

"Your time may come, but for now, I'm relying on you to look after your ma and brothers," Pa had replied.

I knew better than to say anything. Ma ruled her roost like a sharp-beaked hawk, and if I had suggested going with Pa into the army, she would have locked me in a broom closet. As it was, Pa and a couple of other men marched down the aisle and solemnly wrote their names in the muster book. I slithered down to the end of the bench, got to my feet, and made my way over to Pa's side.

"Son?" Pa asked, gazing down at me with surprised eyes.

"I spoke with Captain Harrington," I explained. "Mr. Lincoln needs drummers, too. I won't get myself any bonus, but I'll be one less worry for Ma."

Pa turned and gazed at Ma. She was already turning red, and if we had not been in church, she probably would have flown off the bench, grabbed my ear, and dragged me home.

As it was, she waited until the service was over. Then she marched up and stared down at me with furious eyes.

"William J. Johnston, Junior!" she cried. "What do you think you're doing?"

"Joining up, Ma," I said, taking her hands.

"You're too young and too small. I won't have it," she declared. "You're hardly more than a baby."

"Elizabeth," Pa said, "you haven't looked too closely at him lately. He's outgrown short pants. You didn't see him beating that drum. He stood as stiff and tall as any soldier I've seen. It was as if he were born for the task."

"Lord knows he's not much of a cutter," James said, joining us.

"Will, I can't bear the thought—" Ma began.

"Ma," I said, tightening my grip on her hands. "I want to go. I wanted to before. I don't think I could stand it, watching Pa and the others march off and leave me behind."

"He's his father's son," Pa said, grinning.

"I've always known that," Ma confessed. "Well, maybe the two of you can keep each other from harm. Somebody will have to. Neither one of you has the sense to stay home."

"Thanks," I said, throwing my arms around her and hugging her so tightly that the air left her lungs.

"See you write," she warned. "Try to keep up with your lessons. And Willie, if you let those rebels shoot you, I'll pound on you from here to heaven and back again."

"I'll just turn sideways," I promised. "That way I can hide behind a tree."

"That way you can hide behind a pencil," James said.

Charley, who had stood quietly all that time, took to laughing at that thought. He was, in fact, still laughing the first day of December when Pa and I told him goodbye at the depot.

"We're bound for Virginia now," I boasted as I lifted the drum onto my shoulder and stepped aboard the train.

"Well, we have a stop or two first," Captain Harrington said, nudging me along toward an empty seat. "But we'll be there soon enough."

I erased the grin from my face and waved a final goodbye to Ma, James, and Charley. There were others out there, too—friends, teachers, and neighbors. I nodded to each one I recognized. Then I took my place beside a window. Pa settled in beside me, and the train shuddered. Snowflakes began to fall as we rumbled southward past mountains that suddenly seemed more precious and beloved than ever. For the first time, my stomach knotted, and I wondered if I would ever see them, my mother, or my brothers again.

WE WERE WHOLE DAYS on one train after another, heading south. I lost track of time and distance. After a while I didn't even know where we were. The small stove the conductor lit to heat the car couldn't hold off the gnawing cold, and I wished I had brought along one or two of Ma's quilts.

"Move over some," Pa suggested.

I slid over, and he wrapped his big arm around my shoulders. A little later a lady passenger offered us a wool blanket.

"I'm sort of old for this, don't you think?" I asked Pa when he tucked the blanket under my chin.

"Well, I'm not so sure," he replied. "I guess you think that since you decided to be a soldier, you can't be my boy anymore."

"It's not that, Pa," I told him. "I'm glad you came along."

"Came along? As I recall, I joined first."

"I mean that we'll be together. Maybe I won't make so many mistakes that way. I don't want the others thinking I'm still a child, though."

"I'm not wiping your nose, Willie," Pa pointed out. "Anyway, those other fellows are doing the same thing. I just thought maybe you'd feel a hair more comfortable knowing who was next to you. I know I do, son."

He gave me one of those half grins of his, and I laughed. Glancing behind me, I saw Captain Harrington sandwiched between a couple of fellows from Lyndon. He appeared more than a little ill at ease.

The cold got worse each night. Neither Pa nor the blanket kept my toes from freezing once the sun went down. There were cracks in the sides of the car, and not all the windows fit their frames. I judge some glaciers were never as cold as that car, and I found myself wishing us south. I read once that it never snowed there, and that notion alone was enough to hurry us to Richmond.

We eventually arrived at Washington. It was snowing there, too, and I wasn't the only one to notice.

"I hope they've found us a good warm hotel," Pa said.

"Hotel?" Captain Harrington cried. "You are recruits. You will be lucky to find a tent. Now, get to your feet!" the captain barked. "Beat assembly, drummer!"

His words carried an edge now, and I gazed at him in surprise. There wasn't a hint of the old, relaxed Captain Harrington. I yawned, drew out my sticks, and tapped out the call. Pa and the other recruits stumbled to their feet, took what few possessions they had brought with them, and followed the captain out of the car and onto the wooden plank platform of the depot.

"We'll soon be at Camp Griffin," Captain Harrington explained. "You might as well start behaving like soldiers. You don't look like soldiers, I know, but once we have you properly outfitted and trained, you will."

Myself, I thought the others appeared presentable enough. Compared with some of the soldiers lounging around the depot or on the streets beyond, our little band was military perfection. As a whole, the men were close to six feet tall, and hard work had honed each muscle. Me, I was the runt of the lot, being youngest and a drummer, too. Even so, some of the soldiers we passed weren't too much taller. The army had a general or two who didn't stand five foot six. I read about that in *Harper's Weekly*.

We joined the Third Vermont at Camp Griffin, one of the countless sprawling cities of tents that covered the heights overlooking the Potomac River. Our first stop was the regimental surgeon's tent. He ordered us inside one at a time, starting with Pa. I went last.

I confess the whole business made me a little nervous. Each man walked into that tent and disappeared. When my turn came, I picked up the drum and stepped inside. A somber-faced man in a white coat eyed me sourly and ordered me to set the drum beside the door.

"You the last?" he asked.

"Yes, sir," I replied, trying to stiffen my back and stretch myself taller.

"Does your mother know you're here?"

"Yes, sir," I replied. "Pa's here, too." I gazed around at the tent. A cabinet full of pill jars lined one wall, and there were stacks of papers everywhere. A second door on the far end explained the mysterious disappearance of the others.

"You must be Johnston, Willie," the doctor said, gazing hard into my eyes. "Blue eyes. Fair hair. Any lingering diseases? Amputations?"

"No, sir," I said, showing him my fingers. "I still have both ears, although Ma's lengthened the right one an inch or so."

"She has, eh?" he asked, laughing as he scribbled something in his notebook. "All right. Strip."

"Sir?"

"Peel your clothes, boy. You don't expect me to examine you through a wool jacket, do you?"

I hesitated, but he placed his hands on his hips and grunted. I pulled off my shoes, pants, jacket, and shirt.

"Everything," he muttered impatiently.

"Everything?" I gasped.

"Son, I don't expect you have webbed feet or a tail, but the army expects me to make sure anyway."

I frowned. I shared an attic with two brothers, and in the summer I swam buff naked with friends outside town. Still, I wasn't too eager to bare myself in front of a stranger.

"I hate to hurry you, Willie, but the sooner we get finished, the sooner you can get some clothes back on," he whispered. "Trust Doc Jones, won't you?"

He rested a hand on my shoulder, and I shook off the worst of my embarrassment. Finally I stepped out of my drawers.

"Height," he muttered.

Before I could reply, he backed me against an upright wooden plank, straightened my head, and made a mark on the board with his pencil.

"Four feet, ten inches," he said. "And a half, maybe," he added, reading my disappointment. "Boots will make you taller, of course."

"Of course," I agreed.

He pointed to a set of scales. I hopped across the cold ground and stepped up, and he shifted some weights until a bar balanced.

"Eighty-four pounds," Doc Jones observed. "They must have starved you on that train to get you so skinny. You be sure to come by the officers' mess every day or so. I'll save you something. I don't believe there's a man in this regiment who can cook!"

"I can fry an egg," I boasted. "And boil potatoes."

"Well, we don't get too many of either," he said, poking my side. "Ever had a fit?"

"No, sir."

"Do your bowels move freely?"

I nodded.

He tapped my knees, examined my elbows, and took a good look at my toes.

"Anything wrong?" I asked as he scribbled notes in his book.

"No, son, you've got all your parts. Some of them could do with a scrubbing, and I wish you had a little more meat on you."

"Pa always says it's the hungry wren that will dig deepest for a worm," I declared.

"I believe you'll do, Willie Johnston," the doctor said. "Grab your clothes and slip through that door there to the quartermaster. He'll get you properly outfitted."

"Yes, sir," I said, slipping into my drawers, grabbing my clothes, and hurrying toward the back door.

I didn't have half the trouble with Dr. Jones that I had with the quartermaster. He was a big, round-faced man who joked about my size and laughed at the goose bumps spreading across my nearly frozen back. He finally tossed me some stockings ten sizes too big. The uniform pants would have fit Pa, and the tunic stretched down to my ankles.

"Don't you have anything else?" I asked.

"Questioning my authority, boy?" he barked.

"No," I replied. "Just your eyesight."

The quartermaster got all red and puffed up, and he

was about to march out from behind his counter when Captain Harrington came in.

"Sergeant, what's this?" the captain asked, taking the tunic from my trembling fingers. "He can't wear this! He needs to use his hands. Find him a smaller size."

"Yes, sir," the quartermaster said, scrambling around. In short order he located a uniform that was still big, but I could hem the pants legs myself and shorten the sleeves. Suspenders would take care of the rest.

I got myself dressed, collected my discarded clothes, and followed the captain outside. Calvin Stebbins was waiting there with a grin on his face. My drum rested beside his feet.

"Cal?" I asked.

"Drummer Johnston, I'm detailed to guide you to Company D," Cal told me.

"Where's Pa?" I asked Captain Harrington.

"He'll serve with Company B," the captain explained. "I'm sorry, son, but they already had a drummer. Company D needs one."

"But . . ." I began.

"You know a lot of the boys, Willie," Cal whispered. "Lots of 'em's youngsters like us. It's mostly old gray beards in B."

"Johnston," the captain said, turning me toward the smaller tents of the soldier camps. "You might as well know that a soldier follows orders. You go where you're needed. It might ease your concerns, though, to know that I am commander of Company D."

I stared up at him, nodded slightly, and left with Cal. It didn't make me feel a bit better. The captain knew that Pa expected me to serve with him. I had a sour taste in my mouth about the train trip, and now I had a battle just getting a uniform that would fit. The only kind words I'd heard since joining the regiment had come from Doc Jones, and they were pitiful small compensation for treating me like a prize hog on market day.

Things improved some once Cal led me to his tent.

"Not him!" Orlando Stevens complained when I slipped through the flap and faced my tentmates.

"Welcome to Camp Griffin, Willie," his younger brother Russell said, gripping my frozen hand. "Get this boy closer to the stove, brothers. He's cold as ice."

"I heard the cap growl at that quartermaster about keeping him waiting on a uniform," Cal muttered as he buttoned the flap. "I'd introduce you around, Willie, but I think you know about everybody."

In truth, I did. Besides Russ and Orlando, Calvin Stevens was there, too. The Stevens brothers were all about five foot seven or eight, and they had similar features. Calvin, who everybody called Blackie because of his dark hair, was the middle one. Lando, at twenty, was oldest. He had sandy brown hair and sported the beginnings of a mustache. Russ was eighteen, and he had gray, serious eyes. He reminded me of my brother James.

Moses Torrence, a seventeen-year-old from Melburne; Horace Partlow, a nineteen-year-old from the little town of Holland; and Silome Persons, an old man of twenty from Morgan, also called the conical tent home.

"There are times when eight bodies are a nuisance," Cal observed, "but never on a cold night. We do have to explain about spoke sleeping."

"What?" I asked.

"Each fellow puts his head toward the stove and his feet to the wall," Russ told me. "That way everybody gets some of the warmth. I'll warn you. Tent sleeping takes some getting used to, particularly the smell. But you ought to have a look at some of the other camps if you think we're having a hard time. There are outfits sleeping in wedge tents. They have to sleep spoon style."

"Spoon style?" I asked, scratching my head. "That anything like spoke style?"

"No," Cal said, shuddering. "In a wedge tent, the first man puts his head toward the door. The next puts his feet. There are six men in those tents, and each one has his nose at his tentmate's feet. That's a pleasant thought now, isn't it?"

"The real fun comes when somebody needs to turn," Lando said, shaking his head. "Everybody has to do it at the same time or you can have yourself some serious accidents."

"So you see, we Vermont boys are making out fine," Cal told me. "We have room to move around, and our little stove here keeps us from freezing."

"There's a price to all this high living," Lando observed. "Our stove has an appetite for wood. So whenever we're not drilling or doing picket duty, we're out gathering and chopping logs. You'll take a turn, too, Willie."

"I expect to do my share," I replied.

"Now, who's hungry?" Lando asked.

"I am," I shouted, and the others cried out their agreement. I then had a chance to learn the real merit of having a stove in your tent. Besides keeping us warm, it allowed us the chance to cook our own rations.

"We're issued bread, salted beef or pork, beans, and even vegetables sometimes," Cal explained as Moses dragged over a rations box.

"He's a regular genius," Russ said, nodding at Moses.

"I like to cook," Moses said, taking a slab of bacon from the box. "It's a challenge, considering what they give us, but we do all right."

"We'd better serve Willie a double share," Lando suggested. "You could fit two of him in those trousers."

"I'll fix that directly," I said, sliding the suspenders off my shoulders and pulling off my uniform trousers. Then I took a small sewing kit from the pocket of my civilian trousers and began studying the best way of shortening the waist.

"Forgot your pa's a tailor," Lando said. "You'll be some help to the rest of us. I don't think any of these new pants fit proper."

"I noticed the new uniforms," I said, scratching my ear. "When you left Saint Jay, you wore gray."

"That wasn't too convenient, as things turned out," Lando explained. "Some of the regiments wore gray at Bull Run, and our own men mistook them for rebels. We got directed to make the change. Some got to keep their old clothes and dye them blue. We seven all got new Union Army issue. Considering the quality, I suspect somebody's making a fine profit off those uniforms, Willie. I never got anything from your pa so poorly made."

I examined the fabric. It was pitifully thin, and the stitching was uneven.

"Looks like I'll keep busy mending," I told them.

While I worked on my new trousers, Moses transformed odds and ends from the ration box into a regular feast. He was a magician! Our dinner looked truly inviting, and it tasted even better.

"You can thank Cal for the vegetables," Russ explained as I handed Moses my empty plate.

"He's got a talent for *discovering* vegetables," Moses added. "He goes out on water details, and he brings back a full bucket in one hand and a flour sack filled with carrots or greens in the other. He even discovered an apple pie one day."

"Farmers hereabouts aren't any too happy," Lando said, laughing. "Colonel Hyde tells 'em he can't find any evidence, though."

"There isn't any," Russ noted. "We eat every crumb."

After eating, I helped Russ scrape the plates and clean up. Then our corporal, George Washington Washburn, brought over the rest of my equipment.

"Don't worry about all this other gear," Cal advised, stowing it beside the door. "It's these blankets you need tonight."

"Fetch the rubber one," Lando told Cal. "Now, watch close, Willie. We can't be doing this for you every night."

I watched carefully as Lando and Cal rolled the rubber blanket out onto the hard ground.

"This goes down first," Cal explained. "It will keep the wet out. Most of it, anyway. We're lucky not to be camped in a swamp. Some of the companies have water in their tents."

"When we first got here, we spread out grass and leaves," Lando said, pointing to the residue beneath our feet. "If we ever get some decent weather, we'll cut some more grass and add a layer. That warms things considerably."

"Anyway, you have three blankets, Willie," Cal noted. "Keep two below and one on top. That may seem odd, but trust us. It's a lot colder underneath than it will be on top."

"Thanks," I told them. "You ever need a favor in return, just ask."

"Oh, you'll earn your way," Moses insisted. "We each of us does."

"Sure," Cal agreed. "Wait until the weather breaks, and we get visitors. You won't even have to discover anything. Ladies from Washington and Georgetown come out here with baskets of fruit, pies, cakes, you name it. They always have some treat for the child soldiers."

"I'm no child," I insisted.

"Well, you're no hairy-lipped sour apple of a captain, either," Lando insisted.

"Act little when we get visitors," Cal advised. "One young fellow in Company E got himself a new coat from a young lady. A real warm one, too."

"The coat or the lady?" I asked.

"Both, the way I heard it," Lando cackled.

"Never turn down a kindness, Willie," Russ whispered a little later when we took to our blankets. "You wait and see if there isn't enough hardship. Once the snows melt and we go back to drilling all the time, you'll get so you welcome a fever for the rest it earns you."

I saw the truth of his words in his eyes, and I took it to heart.

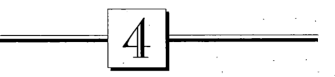

I WAS ROUSED a little short of six o'clock that next morning by a dark-haired fellow in his early twenties.

"You, Johnston," he said, shaking me half to death. "Come along. It's time to beat out reveille."

I yawned and plunged my head back into a blanket.

"Now!" the fellow shouted. He dragged me to my feet, laughed some, and gave my rump a resounding slap.

"Why did you do that?" I asked, rubbing away the sting.

"It's how you get babies breathing, ain't it?" he asked. "I'm Wheeler, the fifer. Get yourself dressed, grab the drum, and come on out. The whole company's bound to be late if we're not on time!"

I shook myself awake, threw on my shirt, and grabbed my drum.

"Willie, you forgot something, didn't you?" Russ asked.

"Eh?" I asked, gazing around at my bedding.

"Boots will help some, but you'd be a little conspicuous without your pants."

I gazed at my bare knees and chuckled. I set the drum back down, pulled on my trousers, slid the suspenders over my bony shoulders, and pulled on my boots. Then I grabbed the drum and hurried outside.

"You know the call?" Wheeler asked as he led me along toward the end of the line of tents.

"Learned it once, but I don't recall it any too well."

"Then listen good. A fife won't wake anybody. Your drum will have to do the trick."

He hummed the tune, and I listened attentively. Then he motioned for me to begin, and I tapped out the reveille command. All around me other drummers were doing the same, and the sounds of drums echoed down toward the river and filled the air with a martial rhythm.

"Now what?" I asked as the men stumbled out of their tents. Some managed to dress themselves, but as many as half remained in their shirts. Some of the soldiers emerged wrapped in blankets.

"You did that just fine," a tallish man in his early thirties announced as he stopped beside us. He buttoned up his tunic, and I recognized immediately the shoulder boards of an officer.

"This is our lieutenant, Erastus Buck," Wheeler explained.

"I'm Willie," I told the lieutenant, offering my hand. "Willie Johnston."

"Welcome to Camp Griffin, Johnston," Lieutenant Buck replied. He did not shake my hand. Instead he drew out a small book from his pocket. "Give them another beat, drummer," he instructed. "And tomorrow make certain you're here on time. Captain Harrington doesn't like to hear another drum before our own beats reveille."

"Yes, sir," I replied, stiffening my back.

Lieutenant Buck stood us opposite the men on what he explained was the color line, where the flags were displayed. That morning no one brought out a flag. It was cold, damp, and misty. I immediately regretted not wearing my tunic because the wind bit right through my shoulders. The lieutenant called out names from his little book, and each man announced his presence. Two or three didn't respond, and one of the corporals explained they were on the sick list.

"The Third's had its fair share of sick," Wheeler whispered.

Once he completed the roll call, Lieutenant Buck dismissed the men and set about making his morning report.

"Want my help, Lieutenant?" Wheeler asked.

"You show our new drummer around," Buck replied. "Get it done fast, though. We'll want breakfast call made on time."

"Come on," Wheeler urged, dragging me behind him. He then devoted half an hour to explaining the camp layout. The officers occupied larger, square-walled tents with peaked tops at the end of a long line of conical soldier tents. Wheeler also showed me the regimental headquarters, the guard stations, and most important, the sinks.

"Everybody finds his way down here," the fifer said, laughing as a tallish fellow in bare feet hurried past us. The regiment had constructed rough latrines in a long line on the fringe of our camp. Another area was devoted to washbasins, and several men shaved off whiskers or washed themselves there. A third area was reserved for dumping garbage. The place had a terribly foul smell.

"There's not much privacy," I observed, noting that the men pretty much crowded together as they relieved themselves.

"I suppose you'd prefer an officer's privy," Wheeler

said, laughing as he stepped up to the rail and dropped his pants.

Actually, I would have. But I found out pretty quickly that the only thing in the army lower than a private was a drummer. We did not, in fact, rate at all. I wasn't even listed on the muster book, and I generally found myself at the end of every line.

"Come on," Wheeler said, making a place for me at the rail. "You can't wait for someone to give you an engraved invitation. Get up here and tend to business. You have to hurry and beat the breakfast call."

I reluctantly tended to nature's call. I sensed a hundred eyes on me, though, and it felt peculiar.

"Sleep all right, son?" Pa asked, making room for himself at my side. "Here, you might want this."

He handed me half a sheet from a newspaper, and I grinned my thanks.

"It's a little hard to get used to," I told him.

"I spoke to Colonel Hyde about moving over to Company D, but he wouldn't allow it," Pa explained. "So I suppose we won't see too much of each other."

"I guess not," I said, frowning. "Don't worry about me, though. Cal Stebbins and the Stevens boys are sharing their tent with me."

"You'll do fine, Willie. Probably grow as tall as I am by midsummer."

"Not on army food," I grumbled.

He laughed then, and I decided that as long as we could laugh in a latrine, we'd both fare all right.

I had to hurry to the color line to make the breakfast call on time. Afterward, I stumbled back to the tent.

"Get something to eat," Wheeler told me. "Then dress yourself properly. Button everything, and put on a cap. That might make you look a hair older. How old are you anyway? Not more than fourteen."

"Not quite twelve," I confessed.

"Children," Wheeler said, sighing. "I'm twenty-four, and I thought I was young. Just what the company needs, another PF."

Wheeler departed, and I stepped inside the tent. Moses was spreading a strange green paste onto flat army biscuits. He handed me one.

"We call it peas on a trencher," Cal explained. "In polite company."

I grinned. It had a little taste to it, but the biscuit was hard, and the peas were cold. I barely got it down my gullet, and I had to gulp down two cups of boiled coffee to get it to stay there.

"Saw you got the guided tour," Russ said, digging my cap out of the pile of equipment heaped beside the door. "We stand inspection around eight, but you'll need to look your best when you beat the sick call. Lieutenant Buck likes to send somebody to the surgeon with the sick men. He's been sending Wheeler. Now I imagine he'll dispatch you."

"Send the most useless fellow in the company, eh?" I asked.

"Not exactly," Russ said, grinning.

"But close," I muttered. "By the way, what's a PF?"

"Peach fuzz," Russ said, reddening.

"They call us that sometimes," Cal said, shaking his head. "Not with kind intentions, either. And it's usually some fellow like Jace Wheeler who only has a few years on us."

"And nothing close to a beard," Russ added.

"Anyhow, you just stand tall and proud when they say

that, Willie," Cal urged. "We sort of call ourselves *fuzzies*. The whole company's on the young side, after all. Once we get into battle, they'll stop snickering."

I kind of took to the name myself. It made us all that much more determined to do each task better. At sick call, my tentmates and I stood at attention in full uniform, and even Lieutenant Buck nodded with approval.

"Johnston," he said once he had given approval for three men to see the surgeon. "You take them down to Doc Jones. Make certain you get this receipt signed for them. And if the doc says they're fit, bring them back here directly."

"Yes, sir," I said, giving him a crisp salute.

"Fuzz," Wheeler mumbled under his breath. I gave him a scowl and took charge of the sick men. They knew better than I did the fastest way to the hospital tent, and I had trouble keeping up, much less leading the way. Two were suffering from bowel problems, and the doc waved them toward his orderly. The third man had a festering cut on his leg.

"You should have seen me earlier," Doc Jones told the man. "This could be serious."

After directing the man inside the tent, the doctor turned toward me.

"You look like a regular soldier now, Willie," he declared.

"Like a drummer, anyway," I replied. "I'd need promotion to merit a private's respect."

"Don't let them bother you, son. Do your duty, be respectful, and even the sourest among them will come along. Now, it's too late to snatch you something from the mess, but I believe I have something in my pocket you can make use of."

He drew out three sticks of candy and pressed them into my hands.

"Thanks, Doc," I said, grinning.

"I'll always have something of the sort for you youngsters," Doc Jones explained. "This should make the misery more digestible and the monotony almost tolerable. Does us all good to see a shine in the eyes of a drummer."

"Yes, sir," I agreed.

Back with the company, I turned over the candy to Moses.

"You should keep one stick just for yourself," he advised.

"No, we share in this tent. Isn't that what you told me?"

"Well, Willie, so long as you keep making discoveries like this, we'll be happy to share the work, the cold, and the smell," he told me.

I used what time remained to fetch kindling for the stove. Cal and Lando were splitting logs, and although I offered to take a turn at the ax, I don't believe either quite trusted me to keep all my toes and still do any damage to those tough Potomac logs.

At eight o'clock I beat the fourth call of the day, guard mount. Captain Harrington inspected the company this time, and he generously meted out complaints. He told Cal to stand straight, and he criticized Blackie Stevens for a smidgen of rust on his rifle.

"Your weapon is the most critical piece of equipment you possess!" the captain growled. "You're useless as a soldier without it. I don't want to see another rifled musket with a trace of tarnish, much less rust! Soldier, you'll stand an extra turn at guard until that rifle shines!"

Lieutenant Buck noted the punishment. Several other men were also assigned extra details. In general, we other fuzzies passed without notice.

While a guard detail marched off to take its posts, Lieutenant Buck nudged my shoulder.

"Beat assembly for drill," he ordered.

I remembered that call, and Wheeler didn't have to help me begin. Those Company D men not assigned other duty lined up and began the long tiresome drilling that marked daily camp life. Wheeler and I took our places at the head of a column, and we played as Company D marched up and down a nearby field. It was cold and wet, and Wheeler told me Captain Harrington wouldn't keep us out long. He didn't.

"Dismiss the men," he told Lieutenant Buck. "They can police the camp until dinner."

"Thank you, sir," Buck replied. He then motioned for me to beat my drum, waved for me to stop, and ordered the company dismissed.

We fuzzies resumed our various camp duties. For me, that meant collecting more kindling. Later I mended tears in my tentmates' clothes. They, in turn, showed me how to stow my equipment. I left only long enough to beat out "roast beef," as the dinner meal call was known.

Moses prepared a stew, and for the first time since leaving Saint Jay, I was actually full. He topped the meal by passing out pieces of my stick candy. He took great pains to explain to everyone that I had provided the treat.

The remainder of that day, like all others, consisted of drumming the different calls and tending to the miscellaneous duties of a company musician. The calls included dress parade, a regimental assembly late each afternoon when the colonel addressed us personally. Cal explained that we usually drilled afterward, but the various companies had churned the field into a bog, and the colonel declined to send us out in the mud again.

Supper call announced the day's third meal. After night fell, I beat tattoo, a final roll call; and taps, signaling all soldiers not posted to guard detail to return to their tents, douse lights, and cease all noise. Most of us rolled out our blankets, stripped down to our underclothes, and tried to find a good night's sleep. Fortunately only Lando among my tentmates snored. Unfortunately he had a habit of falling right to sleep, and anyone who didn't was treated to his bearlike grunts and growls.

We passed all of December, January, and February at Camp Griffin, alternately freezing and drilling. Sometimes we did both. In January Will Currier, a twenty-eight-year-old farmer from Brighton, was promoted to sergeant. He assumed many of Lieutenant Buck's daily tasks. With half of my tentmates from his hometown, you might have suspected the fuzzies would get better treatment.

"Curry's hoping to become an officer," Lando declared. "I don't expect him to let much pass."

Those winter months went by slowly for me. I tried to stay busy, but it wasn't always possible. At the slow times, especially when a blizzard tormented us in late January, I grew homesick. Sometimes I smuggled myself over to Company B and spent the night with Pa.

"Maybe I should speak with the colonel again," Pa suggested. "A lot of boys are winning discharges and going back home."

"I didn't come out here to run home," I argued.

"The company needs me. Captain Harrington says a drummer's the heart of his company. He taps out the pulse so the men know what to do."

On good days, when the regiment drilled together, I had a chance to pass some time with Julian Scott, the fifer artist. He was still sketching everything in sight, and he offered me a portrait to send Ma for Christmas. That drawing showed me beating the drum at guard mount, and I think it made me appear older. Julian also sketched us at other, less favorable moments. He showed us pranking the officers, playing cards, or washing ourselves at the sinks. That last drawing helped kindle a stove.

While the officers tolerated a good deal of foolishness from all the men, and from musicians in particular, they expected us to beat each call on time and keep to our guard posts no matter what. I was stationed with Russ and Blackie Stevens the final week of February. Julian and a Groton boy, Will Scott, also manned the spot. A rider approached around midnight, and I nudged Russ. Will Scott, meanwhile, shouldered his rifle and hollered a challenge.

"Whoa, son," the rider cried. "Brigade messenger."

"Password?" Julian demanded.

"I don't have your fool regiment's password!" the rider barked. "Let me pass. I've got dispatches for Colonel Hyde."

"Dismount," Russ suggested. "We better have a good look at you."

The rider howled a curse or two and complained that some Vermonters didn't have the sense to know black from white. He gave Julian his horse's reins, dismounted, and showed us an order signed by General Brooks, the brigade commander.

44

"Pass," Blackie announced, waving Julian and Will away. "It's fine to be careful, but you can take it too far."

"Well, say what you want," Will declared. "I've had my share of adventures on guard duty, and I wouldn't wish 'em on anybody else."

"Now that's sure true," Julian said, laughing. The others thought a moment and broke out into grins. All except Will, who remained deadly serious.

"You don't understand, Willie," Julian said, shaking his head. "Tell him, Will."

"It's a long story," Will began. "But I wager that once you hear it, you won't take guard duty any too lightly.

"We were stationed at the end of a chain bridge last autumn," Will explained. "One of my tentmates had guard duty, but he was fighting some stomach misery, and feeling sorry for the youngster, I took his place. It was a long, dark night, and I hadn't had much rest. A little past midnight I fell asleep. When the relief arrived, I was sleeping. They took me to the provost, placed me under arrest, and the next thing I knew I was tried, convicted, and sentenced to be shot.

"I always knew there was some danger coming from the rebs, but I never expected my own regiment to deliver me up like that," Will said, shuddering as he recalled it. "They were all set to do it, too."

"We went around writing letters," Julian explained.

"You were just worried they might get their Scotts confused," Will argued.

"Anyhow, we sent petitions from the whole regiment and a considerable part of the army to Mr. Lincoln himself," Julian added. "The next thing you know, the president rides down and has a talk with the generals. 'I will not allow the lad to be shot,' Mr. Lincoln told them."

"I got pardoned and returned to duty," Will said, sighing. "But if Mr. Lincoln's carriage had broken down, or he had had trouble finding the brigade, I would sure be dead."

"And that's why some of us take guard duty seriously," Julian noted. "And you boys will, too, if you're smart."

I couldn't speak for the others. I knew I would. Getting killed in a war's one thing. Being shot for neglecting your duties was another.

T HOSE FIRST DAYS OF MARCH a hundred rumors spread through Camp Griffin. Brigade messengers appeared from time to time, and we were all anxious to learn what our new orders might be.

"I joined the army to fight," Lando complained. "They call us the Army of the Potomac. We might as well be the Army of the Connecticut for all the good we're doing. We've lost more men to sick call than the rebs would have killed keeping us out of Richmond!"

Most of us felt the same way. The Third Vermont did suffer considerably from different sicknesses, with a third of the whole regiment down at times that winter. Long days of drill and more drill wore us out, and some of the men debated heading home to get the spring crops in.

"You can't just desert," I insisted when Russ suggested leaving. "You swore an oath."

"Pledged to fight," Russ muttered. "I'll be back before this army moves a dozen miles."

What galled us in particular was the news that the western army under an Illinois general, Ulysses Grant, had smashed the rebel forts in Tennessee and Kentucky. At Fort Donelson Grant bagged a whole rebel army, fifteen thousand soldiers. Now the westerners were driving south toward Mississippi and Alabama.

"Just give us a chance and we'll thrash those rebs," Lando boasted to Colonel Hyde at dress parade the evening of March 9.

"You will soon have that opportunity," the colonel replied. "Tomorrow we break camp and march south."

"Hooray!" the men shouted, tossing their caps in the air.

We took down our tents, packed our equipment, and prepared for the move that night. Jason Wheeler and I roused the men an hour early that next morning, and Captain Harrington pointed out the wagons in which we would stow our tents, stoves, and heavy equipment. All our clothes, weapons, canteens, and rations went with us on foot.

"Willie, you can't mean to pack all that," Cal objected when I began stuffing my belongings in a knapsack.

"You must have fifty pounds there!" Russ exclaimed. "Add the drum, and there will be more equipment than drummer."

"Just take what you have to," Cal advised.

He sifted through things, tossing out spare shirts, tin plates, and the like.

"We smuggle the cooking gear into the wagons," Russ told me. "You don't need more clothes than you can wear."

"You won't need all those blankets, either," Cal observed. "Keep the rubber one and a single good one of wool."

"And the rest?" I asked.

"We'll stow them in a wagon for now," Cal explained. "We might be able to swap them for a chicken later on."

With Cal's help, I whittled down my gear to around thirty pounds.

"It's still too heavy," Russ observed. "Toss that spare pair of drawers away, but keep the socks."

"Those are good winter woolens," I argued. "From home. The cotton rags the army provides won't survive a good washing."

"Willie, most of the fellows lost those drawers first thing," Cal declared. "You carry thirty pounds on your back a day or so, and you'll learn anything you don't need this hour, this day, is best left behind."

They were right, of course, but that didn't make it any easier to stomach. I finally trimmed my gear down to twenty pounds, not counting the drum. Once I was fully dressed, with my knapsack strapped onto my back, haversack on my left hip, and canteen on the right, I realized another ounce or two would have overwhelmed me.

"Remember, Johnston," Lieutenant Buck whispered when Wheeler and I took our places at the front of Company D's column, "that drum is vital to the success of this company and the regiment as a whole. See that you are attentive to orders, keep pace with the column, and no matter what, keep that drum at your side."

"Yes, sir," I promised.

Our move south was a disappointment. We crossed the Potomac, but we went no farther than Alexandria, on the southern bank. The little port city, with its steepled churches and fine brick houses, was transformed into a sea of bluecoated soldiers.

"Some say we are headed for the Carolinas," Wheeler whispered as he pocketed his fife. "Others say Florida."

"I don't guess we'll be the Army of the Potomac down there," I observed.

In the end, we erected our tents, drilled, and waited.

We lingered there close to two weeks. Then Colonel Hyde addressed us the morning of March 23.

"The rebels have taken another licking at Kernstown, in the Shenandoah Valley," the colonel noted. "Now it will be our turn to shatter their defenses. We are boarding ship and sailing south to the Virginia Peninsula. It's on to Richmond, boys!"

We stomped our feet and raised a howl, but this time we held on to our hats. Most of us remained skeptical about the new orders. Before the day was out, though, we were marching up gangways and boarding the crazy collection of inland ferries, tugs, and cargo ships that had been leased to transport the Army of the Potomac toward Richmond.

I had never been to sea, and the short voyage out into Chesapeake Bay and down the Virginia coast seemed like an adventure. Some of the men had a rough time of it. The Stevens brothers, all three of them, spent most of the trip hanging over the stern rail, heaving their insides out.

A good part of the regiment sailed on our ship, and Captain Harrington suggested I join the other musicians and practice the drum calls. I located Julian Scott, and he agreed to play the calls with his fife while I tapped them out on my drum.

"We don't really need to practice anymore," Julian told me after we went through each of the calls twice. "After all those weeks of drill, I hear them in my sleep."

"Sure," I agreed. "It's something to pass the time, though, and I think the men like to hear the music."

"Then they're crazy," Julian grumbled. "They'll be hearing these marching calls soon enough, and it won't be to tell them we're going to line up for sick call. There's a fight brewing."

We went through the calls a third time. Then Pa waved to me from the crates stacked behind the ship's foremast.

"Go on," Julian urged. "You've drummed long enough."

I grinned to him, trotted over to the crates, and sat down beside Pa.

"Sounds to me like you know your job," Pa observed.

"I hope so," I said, staring off toward the misty Virginia shore. "I guess we'll be going into battle pretty soon."

"Could be, son," he said, pulling me closer. "You know, Willie, I don't believe I've ever been as proud of you as when you walked over and joined me beside Captain Harrington in the church."

"I suppose it was time I made you proud of something," I said, sighing. "Mostly you've had cause to wish I was somebody else's problem."

"Not so much," he argued. "You get into mischief, I'll admit, but it's the Johnston itch to try new things and test out rules. I did it myself. I trust you'll find more success than your old father's had."

"You've done fair," I told him.

"Not by half," he muttered. "That's not what I wanted to talk to you about, though. If it's a fight that's coming, you'll find yourself on your own. I'll be off with Company B. I know there are good men around you, but they're young themselves. You can't count on them keeping you safe. You'll have to watch out for yourself."

"Don't worry, Pa. Captain Harrington says we drummers will be stretcher-bearers when the real battle comes."

"And who will signal the advance?" Pa asked. "If that's true, why do you boys drill right beside us?"

"I don't know," I said, scratching my ear. "I guess I'll be scared some if we march along and the rebs start shooting at us. I won't run, Pa. Not if I can help myself."

"It's not your running that worries me, Willie. It's how tall you stood up in that church. If people start shooting, you find a rock or a tree to hide behind. Those rebel bullets won't care if you're just a boy. You understand?"

"Yes, sir," I replied. "I'll do my best to shy away from danger."

"I'm not saying you shouldn't do your duty, son, but the army's got scant use for a dead drummer. And you can beat the calls as well from behind a rock as on the top of a hill."

That afternoon as our ship waited its turn to enter Hampton Roads, I thought about what Pa had said. In truth, I hadn't given much thought to a real battle. Mainly I'd been too busy. But if a fight was coming, and everybody said it was, then there would be shooting—and dying. That unsettled me considerably.

My spirits weren't lifted when we entered the anchorage off Fort Monroe. A sea battle had taken place there recently, and the U.S.S. *Cumberland*, a big sailing ship, had been sunk by the rebel ironclad *Merrimack*. The *Cumberland*'s masts still stuck up above water, and a flag bravely flew from one of them. That both saddened and cheered us. I couldn't help thinking about the drowned sailors, but that defiant flag put us in a fighting mood.

The sailors muttered nervously about the dreaded *Merrimack*, but I knew we had our own ironclad now, the *Monitor*. She was a little flat-decked ship with a revolving round cheese box–like gunhouse. I spied the odd ship myself, and Captain Harrington waved his hat at it.

"That's the fool thing that's going to protect us?" Cal asked as he stumbled over beside me. "I hope the good Lord's got a sense of humor. Maybe He'll look down and laugh so hard that He'll feel sorry for the *Monitor.*"

I didn't deem pity necessary. The evil-looking barrels frowning out from the *Monitor*'s gunports were purely inspiring.

Our ship slipped past the *Monitor* and eased up to a landing near one of the fort's long stone walls. Sailors dashed about, tying lines and setting up gangplanks. Then our officers formed the companies. The Third Vermont disembarked in fine order, and once our equipment was unloaded, we passed in and out of Fort Monroe and down the Peninsula toward Richmond.

I didn't find Virginia very hospitable. Our first camp was in a bog, and small armies of mosquitoes and gnats descended on us. The mosquitoes nearly ate me whole. Worse, fevers plagued us so that each morning a new man or two fell out, sick.

We passed almost two weeks in the shadow of the fort, swatting insects and cursing rebels. On April 4 we finally broke camp and marched west, toward Yorktown. The rebs were using the old Revolutionary War trenches to hold us at bay, and the Third Vermont, along with the rest of General Brooks's brigade, was moving out to flank them.

If we had only had to fight rebs, I suppose we would have made short work of the campaign. Our second day on the march, the skies fell in. The wind blew sheets of rain at us, and the ground beneath us began to ooze. I had trouble walking. I would plant one foot, but when I tried to lift the other, the mud would suck my boot right off my foot.

Nights were a regular nightmare. Our equipment wagons were hopelessly bogged down on what passed for a Virginia road, and so we slept in trees, in puddles, or wherever there was space. I managed to cover myself with my rubber blanket, but I was wet through anyway. I could feel mud between my toes, in my ears, stuck to my hair, and just about every other place imaginable. Our rations were miles behind, and we might have starved if Cal hadn't discovered a smokehouse full of hams.

We had ourselves a regular feast, and when the owner, a fine Southern gentleman with white hair and a mustache to prove it, rode out on his horse to complain, Captain Harrington just laughed.

"You brought the war upon yourself, sir," the captain insisted. "Before we have finished here, you are liable to be more inconvenienced than by the loss of a few hams."

"We've smashed Grant in Tennessee," the old man barked. "Joe Johnston is coming out from Richmond soon to chase you infernal Yankees back into the sea. And when the *Virginia* returns, your burning fleet will light the night sky for a hundred miles!"

I didn't understand most of that until later. Cal brought word from a headquarters cook that the rebs had attacked Grant at a place called Shiloh, in Tennessee. The western army had fought the rebs to a stalemate, but the cook said ten thousand men were dead. Then, on April 11, the *Merrimack,* or *Virginia,* as the rebs had renamed her, came out from Norfolk and scattered our fleet.

It seemed like all the news was discouraging. We got closer to Yorktown, but the mud and misery were wearing us down. Colonel Hyde allowed us a morning off, and a third of the regiment marched down to the James River to wash uniforms. Most of us decided to scrub ourselves, too.

I confess we were a sight, four hundred men and boys, stark naked and in plain view of the neighboring houses. A couple of black women brought us cakes of soap.

"You boys don't mind us," one lady said, laughing at some of the fellows' poor attempts at modesty. "We've ben scrubbing white boys most all our lives."

"Kind of surprised some of us, though," a second woman added. "Master Jubal said you Yankees had tails."

Some white girls came by later, and I considered myself fortunate for being short. It didn't take too much water to cover most of me up.

"Must be hard on them," Julian told me as we swam into deeper water. "Their brothers and fathers are probably in the army, and here the enemy's camped right on their doorstep."

I hadn't thought about that. It saddened me some, especially when I saw a little boy about the same age as my brother Charley.

"They could always free their slaves," I told Julian.

"Guess so," he agreed. "Anyway, I think I might make some sketches of them."

"Just don't draw me taking a bath," I grumbled.

That bath turned out to be quite an event. We were in the water maybe half an hour when we heard a loud pop from upriver. Suddenly a big tree on the shore exploded. I heard the pop again, and a spout flew up from the water.

"They're shelling us, boys!" Lieutenant Buck hollered.

I glanced behind me and saw a little scow of a gunboat coming toward us. Men stood on its bow, reloading a cannon.

"That's not civilized, shooting at you in the middle of a bath!" Cal howled. The gunboat threw a third shell at us, though, and I joined the naked charge toward shore. Those girls were still up there, but I didn't much care now. I didn't plan on getting myself shot to pieces!

We soon had our revenge on the gunboat. The boys in Company E had brought their rifles along. They formed a skirmish line and moved out toward the shore. Two well-aimed volleys peppered the gunboat with lead. The gunners abandoned their stations, and the boat swung back toward the main channel.

"Now we can get back to our washing," Cal declared.

We hastily washed most of the mud out of our uniforms, but the whole time we kept a wary watch on the river. I sloshed my way back to camp in my wet uniform, as did most of the fuzzies. We hung up our clothes to dry once we were safely clear of the river. Next day we were back in the mud, as miserable as ever.

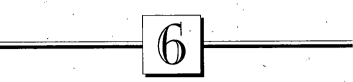

THE THIRD VERMONT broke camp that next morning and headed west again. "On to Richmond," we yelled. But it didn't seem as though we were getting very far along. Each march was worse than the one before, and I came close to cursing. Between the heat and the mud and the miserable rain, Virginia was taking on the look of a godforsaken land. The narrow roads led some men to straggle. Regiments spread out over miles, and the trailing companies sometimes took hours to catch up.

Along the way dozens of slaves flocked to our lines, hoping for protection from their former owners. The year before, at Fort Monroe, a reb officer had appeared under a flag of truce and demanded the return of a runaway slave. General Ben Butler, the fort's commander, had refused. Soon hundreds of slaves were escaping. Some politicians and many generals wanted the slaves sent back, but General Butler had insisted the slaves were contraband, just like cotton or gunpowder. They could be used to aid the rebel cause, too, and he kept them at the fort.

Some Massachusetts regiments backed General Butler with their muskets, and later on President Lincoln him- self stopped the return of runaways. We Thirders were an abolitionist lot from an abolitionist state, and we helped the slaves whenever we could. Some, like the women at James River, refused to leave their plantations. Scores of others poured into our lines, choking the roads and halting our advance. Most of those slaves came with little more than the clothes on their backs. They had no food, inadequate clothing, and no shelter. We distributed what spare blankets and extra food we had, but it was not enough. Slaves kept coming, and we had to shake our heads sadly and pass on by.

I was especially touched by the look of the little children. One morning our entire company gave up its breakfast ration to a crowd of youngsters. Most of them were no bigger than my brother Charley, and it tore at my insides to see them hungry, dressed in rags, and staring stone-faced at the sky. Not one of them, or their mothers or fathers, would ask us for a thing.

"You boys go on fightin'," one white-haired old man urged. "You chastise dem others."

I had always pictured slaves as big strong men picking cotton, but seeing all ages and sizes turned me bitter toward the rebels. I bit my lip and quickened my step.

The Third eventually spread out opposite the rebel works near Yorktown. The town itself looked out on the York River, but we only got near the river once. Cal organized a batch of us into a foraging party, and we collected some oysters in a tidal pool. The rest of the time we dug earthworks, paraded out of range of the rebel guns, and waited for a chance to fight.

"This army has a strange notion of campaigning," Lando complained the night our equipment finally caught up with us. "We rush halfway around Virginia so we can surprise the rebs, and then we sit here, waiting."

We all felt that way. As I helped erect our tent on the soggy Virginia ground, I gazed around at my companions. We were mud-spattered and generally weary. Our hair and clothes were full of lice, and mosquitoes attacked us hourly. Every few days a new man took sick, and the regiment was gradually melting away. We all wished General McClellan would go ahead and attack. Instead he ordered out scouts, sent observation balloons up into the air to look over the reb defenses, and called the other generals to conferences.

The only hint of war was the occasional firing off of a few cannons. Our guns pounded a stretch of the rebel lines, and they shot back later. It was the worst kind of luck to get hit by one of those cannonballs. The gunners were not aiming at anybody in particular, and they caused no real damage. Most times the company nearest our artillery would pass the word up and down the line whenever the gunners went to work, and we would cower in our waterlogged trench or hide behind one of the quartermaster wagons.

Captain Harrington had us up and digging or drilling every morning it wasn't raining, but he mostly let us alone in the afternoons. Some of the men used the time to hunt hogs that had escaped from the neighboring farms. At first the men shot the porkers with their shiny new Springfield rifled muskets, but Colonel Hyde put a stop to that when the rebs began firing cannons in response to what they imagined was an attack.

"Any objection to our hunting with bayonets?" Cal asked.

The colonel just smiled, and the hunting soon resumed. I saw hogs speared with bayonets, shot with handmade bows and arrows, and even trapped in pits.

"I don't suppose it matters how the hog meets his end," Russ observed. "The meat tastes the same."

I had no rifle myself, nor even a bayonet, so I was little use as a hunter. I aided my companions in another way, though. All along the Yorktown line little streams or ravines separated the lines. One afternoon, as I was out gathering kindling for the cook fire on our side of such a stream, I felt a tap on my shoulder. I turned, saw a youngish reb soldier pointing a pistol at my face, and jumped a foot in the air.

"Don't git yerself all stirred up," he urged.

It was the first time I had come face to face with the enemy, and I stood there, wide-eyed, unable to move.

"Yuh won't go yellin' or nothin', will yuh?" he asked. I managed to shake my head, and he stuffed the pistol in his belt. "I come to trade," he added. "I got some good tobacco. Swap it fer coffee."

"I . . . uh . . ."

He shook his head at me and began laughing.

"First time anybody ever took fright from seein' me," he confessed, taking off his cap. He had enormous ears that stood out to each side of his freckled face. "Name's Jeb, short for Jebez, Davis. Now don't go mistakin' me fer our illustrious president, who's not even a close cousin."

"I wouldn't," I assured him. His smile and those immense ears simply overpowered my fear, and I managed to regain my senses. It was pretty hard to be afraid of Jeb. He looked a little older than me, but not much. He wasn't as tall. The tattered legs of his brown trousers stopped an inch shy of his bare feet, and what passed for a tunic had six or seven patches on the right sleeve alone.

"Ain't much to look at, am I?" he asked.

"Not much," I agreed. "But then I'm not so much myself."

"Yuh'd be a drummer, bein' small as yuh are," Jeb observed. "Yanks don't allow youngsters on the fightin' line. I drum myself, but come Christmas, when I turn fourteen, the captain's promised me a musket."

"I'm not yet twelve," I told him. "I don't have much use for tobacco, but I'll pass on word of your offer. We could probably sacrifice some coffee."

"Yuh decide to swap, come back tomorrow morn," he suggested. "I'll be nearby."

"You won't go pointing that pistol at me next time, will you?"

"Naw, I don't shoot at friends," he assured me. "What's yer name anyhow?"

"Willie," I told him. "Willie Johnston. From Vermont."

"I'm a Georgian myself," Jeb explained. "Yuh keep yer head down, Willie. And don't tell no officers. They frown on such doin's."

I nodded. I glanced a moment back toward our lines, and Jeb vanished like a puff of smoke. I shrugged my shoulders, collected some sticks, and headed back to camp.

My tentmates were overjoyed to learn of Jeb's offer, and I swapped a pound of coffee for several twists of tobacco that next morning. Jeb handed me a list of wants, and I returned to camp and began scrounging. With a little help from my tentmates I came up with five blankets, three lengths of cloth, seven razors, twelve pairs of shoes, and two more pounds of coffee.

"That reb wants just about everything but powder and lead," Russ noted.

"I don't suppose we'd want to trade that," I said.

"That'll come later," Lando said, frowning. "When the fighting gets going. Meanwhile, I don't favor swapping a man the lead he can mold into a bullet that can kill me." We all agreed.

In truth, Jeb and his company were far more interested in coffee, razors, shoes, and cloth. Already the South was running short. Virginia was full of tobacco, though, and cut off from markets. The Army of the Potomac, over a hundred thousand strong now, had eaten just about every pea and carrot between Hampton Roads and Yorktown, so vegetables carried a high value on our side of the stream. I got plenty of tobacco, several fine smoking pipes, and every kind of vegetable available on the Virginia Peninsula.

I hoped things would remain quiet along the line because I wanted my visits with Jeb to continue. The trading died down after the first day, but I went back to the stream that next day even though I had nothing but soap and a little salt to trade. The youngest of my tentmates was seventeen, and I enjoyed sharing time with somebody close to my own age. We talked quite a while. Then someone tossed a rock into the stream, and Jeb grew solemn at that signal.

"Cain't stay any longer," he declared. "Don't yuh come back, either, Willie. Yer officers've started sendin' out pickets, and the sentries are jittery. Liable to shoot anybody."

"I guess a battle's coming."

"Ain't had one in a time, Willie. S'pose it was bound to be. Yuh watch out, hear?"

"You, too," I replied. "You make a big target with those ears of yours."

"Most ever'thing else o' mine runs to the small side," he said, laughing as he gazed down at his toes. "I wouldn't even much care if they shot an inch or so off my ear. I wouldn't favor losin' a leg, though. My brother Billy give one up at Manassas."

"Sorry," I said, frowning.

"No matter," Jeb muttered. "Yuh got yer fight to make, and I got mine." There was a new hardness in his eyes, though, and I found myself staring at the pistol in his belt. It didn't seem possible that somebody could be both a friend and an enemy at the same time. But there we were, face to face. Yank and reb.

As I turned to leave, I heard him slither into the brush and disappear. When I returned to camp, Russ ran over and grabbed my elbow.

"Willie, Lieutenant Buck's been asking after you," he whispered. "Get on up to the captain. Something's happening."

I had sensed it the moment I left Jeb. I located my drum, slipped the sash over my shoulder, and hurried to the captain's tent. Jace Wheeler, pale as death, was leaning on a stack of crates beside the flap.

"Johnston, get inside," the little fifer urged.

"You sick?" I asked.

"Inside," he muttered. "Before the captain starts yelling again."

I stepped inside, met Captain Harrington's frowning eyes, and froze.

"Willie, hurry up your firewood gathering hereafter," Lieutenant Buck said, fighting back a grin. "Doesn't do to have our drummer long absent from camp."

"No, it doesn't," Captain Harrington declared. "I want you to beat assembly in five minutes, boy. Meanwhile, dress yourself properly. I won't have the company going into battle like a band of ragged rebels."

"Battle?" I gasped.

"Yes," he barked. "You've kept Wheeler waiting ten minutes already. He almost had to call assembly with that fool fife of his! Children! I wish I had a few grown men in this command."

I thought to point out that Wheeler was better than twenty years old, but it's not wise to pour oil on a smoldering fire. The captain had always been somewhat nervous, and he was pacing around his tent like a man who had sat down on a hornet's nest. I dashed outside, hurried to my tent, and began throwing on my uniform.

"What is it, Willie?" Cal asked.

"We going someplace?" Blackie cried.

"Battle," I told them. "I'm beating assembly as soon as I can find my canteen."

"Lord almighty," Cal said, scrambling around in a frantic effort to locate his cartridge box. "Lord almighty."

"Johnston!" Sergeant Currier howled. "Johnston!"

I slung my canteen over my shoulder, buttoned up my pants, and fastened my two top tunic buttons.

"I'm here, Will," I said as I dragged myself out of the tent.

"Button yourself," he scolded. "And don't address me by my Christian name."

"Sorry, sergeant," I said, staring at my toes.

"Well, don't stand there like a schoolboy caught with a frog in his pocket," the sergeant said, grinning slightly. "See if you can finish dressing and get up to the color line before the rest of us are old and gray. Call assembly."

"Yes, sergeant," I replied. I did as ordered and hurried to my station. Captain Harrington and Lieutenant Buck were already there. The captain was fidgeting, slapping his gloves against his knee, and babbling to himself. Lieutenant Buck appeared calm. He nodded to me, and I took my station, pulled out my sticks, and beat assembly. Seconds later I heard Julian Scott's fife. Company E was assembling as well. Across the way, F and K stood to arms.

There was a rare urgency in the air, and the men quit their usual grumbling and formed lines. Some trotted over in their shirts, but Lieutenant Buck and the sergeants hurried them back to their tents. In short order the whole company, or at least that part of it that wasn't sick, lined up and awaited orders.

"Boys," Captain Harrington finally said, "we have the honor of leading the regiment into action!"

"Hurrah!" Sergeant Currier shouted.

The others added a faint echo.

"General Smith himself is waiting for us," Lieutenant Buck added. "Here we have been at war close to a year, and somebody's finally seen the sense of putting us into action. Shall we disappoint the general?"

"No!" we roared.

"Captain?" Lieutenant Buck asked.

Captain Harrington took his cue. He formed the men into a column, and we began marching. Wheeler and I stood at the head of the company, beating a steady pace. My sticks pounded the drum, and my feet sloshed along the muddy road. The captain had slipped back down the file, but Lieutenant Buck remained nearby.

"That's it, Willie," he told me. "Keep the pace steady. You're doing just fine, son. Just fine."

I tried to smile. I tried to swell up with the kind of

pride I had back in Saint Jay, beating the drum as the captain called for volunteers. I felt the eyes of the whole regiment on my back, though, and I remembered what the officers had told me a thousand times.

"A drum is the heartbeat of the army."

Mostly, though, I found myself thinking about Jeb and his crippled brother. I tried to muster the rage I had felt when we had fed the slave children our breakfast. I couldn't do it. Instead I glanced sideways toward the Company B camp, hoping Pa might be assembling, too. His company was marching off to the right, though, and I had no chance to see him.

I was off to battle, alone, with only Wheeler and his fife for company. I was nervous and practically scared to death. What a crazy notion it was, joining the army, going to war! I shook off the image of Saint Jay, of Ma and James and Charley. Instead I concentrated on the slope just ahead and the swampy ground that lay beyond.

"Lord, help us," I prayed as we continued onward. "Lord help us."

A T A SLIGHT RISE OF GROUND overlooking the swamp we came upon a group of officers on horseback. I recognized Colonel Hyde right off. A fine-looking man with a narrow mustache, stumpy beard, and receding hairline rode beside him.

"Well, so this is the Third!" he shouted. "Boys, look at that swamp. I have to know if anybody's back there. You have to find out."

"We will, General Smith," Colonel Hyde replied. "Captain Harrington, form your command."

"Yes, sir," the captain muttered.

As Captain Harrington waved the men into a line, I stood staring at the general. Here was the famous "Baldy" Smith, a Vermonter like me, who was now in command of a whole division.

"Awhile back Little Mac himself was up here," Julian Scott told me. Companies E and K were forming a reserve, and Julian had managed to escape for a few moments.

"General McClellan?" I whispered. "Is it going to be a regular battle like Bull Run then?"

"Don't think so," Julian said, motioning toward the nearby artillery batteries. Only half were manned, and the Fifth Vermont, over to our left, was only sending a few men out as skirmishers.

"Looks like Mac had more important things to do," Wheeler declared. "Has to get some more balloons up maybe."

"Company D, form skirmish line!" Lieutenant Buck shouted then, and I turned rigid.

"No, stay back," Wheeler told me. "That drum won't do much good in a charge. We'll serve as runners and stretcher-bearers."

Running messages from place to place didn't seem so bad. I didn't want to think about stretchers, though. About wounded and dying friends.

"Company F, form skirmish line!" Captain Sam Pingree, their commander, shouted.

I turned to look for Captain Harrington. He was growing pale, and once again Lieutenant Buck took charge of things. Company F raced up and formed a second line.

"It's in your hands, captain," Colonel Hyde said as he waved toward the swamp.

"Yes, sir," Captain Harrington replied.

Those hands seemed awfully nervous to me. Wheeler and I followed the captain as he approached the swampy ground in front of us.

"Beat an advance," the captain instructed.

I began tapping on my drum, and Wheeler blew a tune on his fife. The Company F drummer started playing, and our two lines began to advance. We soon reached a narrow dike, and the companies halted. Lieutenant Buck and half our company cautiously crept across the dike. Others followed. I glanced at Captain Harrington, but he appeared to be in no hurry, so I rushed ahead to be with my tentmates.

"Get back, Willie," Lando growled. "That drum's not going to kill any rebs."

"No, but it can steady the men some," I argued

We crossed the dam and stared at a stream. On the far side a line of earthen mounds rose. That was the rebel line. Company D spread itself out opposite the line while Captain Pingree deployed Company F behind us.

"I don't see a thing," Russ whispered. "Where are the rebs?"

"Maybe they've fallen back to Richmond," I suggested.

"Don't you bet your life on that," Sergeant Currier muttered. "Fix bayonets! Unfasten your waist belts and hold them high! Try not to get your cartridges wet crossing that stream. Be ready to charge."

After days and days of drill, the men responded to orders with a precision that amazed me. I didn't really know what to do with myself, but I decided if there was going to be a fight, I ought to be with my friends. Captain Harrington, who was senior to the other company commanders and thus in charge, hung back. Lieutenant Buck led us into the shallows. Once we started across, Captain Pingree led Company F forward.

"Well, there's no retreating now," Cal remarked. "Not with those F boys and their bayonets behind us."

We were better than halfway across the stream when the first of our cannons opened up on the rebel entrenchments. The shells roared overhead and whined down on the opposite side of the stream. Some exploded over the trenches. Others blasted gaps in the enemy fortifications. More than a few fell harmlessly into the trees back of the rebel line.

The stream was deeper than it had appeared, and I had to swim across fifteen feet or so. Some of the other youngsters did likewise. The older, taller men managed it better. They held their rifles and cartridge belts up to keep them dry. We emerged on the far side, formed up, and advanced.

I saw my first rebels a few minutes later. They swung their rifles out over their earth walls and let loose a fierce volley. I heard the series of pops, and I saw the powder smoke obscure the trench line. Then my ears picked up a buzzing sound like bees flying around.

It seemed for a minute or so that the world stood still. A man here and there fell back as if tipped over by a giant hand.

"Calvin?" Lando called.

Blackie turned toward his brother, and Cal Stebbins turned back as well. Lando gazed out at them with a bewildered stare, dropped to his knees, and fell.

"Lando!" Russ shouted.

I got to him first, though. I had a little bag of bandages, and I knelt down and opened it, hoping to bind Lando's wound. The bandages had gotten soaked crossing the creek, though.

"Don't bother," Sergeant Currier said, helping me back to my feet. "He's past helping."

I stared at Lando's frozen eyes. Their lifeless gaze chilled me to the bone. Lando had two big holes in his chest, and I thought for a moment I was going to be sick.

"Beat the advance, Willie," the sergeant urged. "Let's take that line before we catch a second volley."

I took a deep breath, exhaled, and beat my drum. The men raised a great howl and raced forward. Those whose powder had remained dry fired their rifles. The others used their bayonets.

The rebs rose up and met us, but their colonel, a tall

man brandishing a saber, drew most of our fire. When he went down, the other rebs lost heart, scrambled out of their trench, and fled.

"We showed 'em the price of tangling with the Third!" Moses Torrence shouted.

I rushed back to have another look after Lando, but he was just as dead as before. Russ and Blackie sat beside him, folding his arms across his chest.

"Form up!" Lieutenant Buck shouted. "Form up!"

"Watch him, will you, Willie?" Russ asked.

I nodded, and the surviving Stevens brothers raced to take their place in our thinned-out line. Company F crowded in beside us, and the reserve companies, E and K, crossed the stream. We were now better than two hundred strong, but nobody seemed to know what to do. Captain Harrington appeared surprised that we had made the crossing.

"Wheeler, go back and tell the colonel that we have taken the rebel works," the captain ordered. "Ask him for support."

Wheeler pocketed his fife, nodded to me, and raced back toward the stream. He, too, had to swim a good portion of the way, but he splashed out on the far shore and continued onward.

The action was growing hotter by the moment in the rebel trenches. Off to our left and especially on the right the rebs opened up on us. There were a lot of them, and their fire began knocking men down in twos and threes.

"Where's our support?" Lieutenant Buck shouted.

I turned to look for Captain Harrington, but he had vanished. There was a collection of soldiers cowering behind a large earthen mound, and I hurried over there.

"Willie, for God's sake get down!" Julian Scott shouted.

I stumbled and fell, and his face tightened up. Once I got to my knees, he seemed relieved.

"Thought you dead for sure," Julian said, hauling me along to safety. "Is anybody in command?"

"Don't ask me," I said, gazing around at the confusion. Some of the sergeants managed to gain control of their squads, but fresh batches of rebs popped up everywhere. Our artillery resumed its bombardment, but the gunners were shooting blindly. The rebs began closing in, and their fire peppered our thin line.

"I'll see if I can find an officer," Will Scott volunteered. He no sooner got to his feet than a reb ball struck him in the chest.

"Help me," Julian cried, cradling Will's head. I opened my bandage bag and took out the soggy bandages. With Julian's help I wrapped Will's chest and stemmed some of the bleeding. Then we carried him back to the stream's edge.

"I better fetch my drum," I declared as Julian started into the stream.

"I've got him now," Julian told me. "Go find that fool captain of yours and see if he can get us out of this mess."

I turned back, retrieved my drum, and crawled along the trench, calling for the captain.

"He's back on the far side of the stream," a Company F soldier told me. "Captain Pingree's taken command."

I located Captain Pingree sitting on a nearby flour barrel. A sergeant was bandaging the captain's bloody hand.

"Good, here's a drummer," Captain Pingree said,

grabbing my shoulder with his good hand. "Son, once this fool finishes his handiwork, I want you to beat recall."

"Recall?" I asked.

"Retreat," he said grimly. "If we had a call for run like the devil, I'd suggest that. We're being murdered here, and it's clear no help is coming."

"Yes, sir," I replied.

I waited for the sergeant to finish. Then Captain Pingree nodded, and I began drumming. I never beat that drum half so hard in my whole life. The men began stumbling back, firing off the few dry cartridges they had left. Then the whole lot of us ran back toward the creek.

The only thing that saved us was that the rebs stayed put. If their brave colonel had survived, he probably would have charged after us and killed everyone. I drummed and drummed until Captain Pingree finally grabbed my arm and halfway threw me into motion. The two of us raced along toward the creek. Then he cried out and fell.

His sergeant and I turned back.

"Now this one's going to be hard to explain to the wife," Captain Pingree said, clasping his bloody rump with his good hand. The sergeant laughed, handed me his rifle, and lifted the captain up onto his shoulders. I stumbled along after them.

The stream was a mess. Dead and wounded littered the shore, and soldiers discarded their rifles and cartridge belts as they dived into the water and swam for safety. I helped the sergeant swim Captain Pingree across. Only then did I see Captain Harrington.

"Why did you wait so long to pull the men out of there?" Captain Harrington shouted.

The men muttered a dozen answers, and more than one questioned his courage. There was Sam Pingree, with a hole in his backside and a thumb shot clear off. Who had a right to question Captain Pingree about anything?

I didn't stay around to learn more. Instead I raced over to where Julian Scott was dragging another wounded man ashore. I set down my drum and helped ease the man to dry ground.

"Take care of this for me, will you?" Julian asked, handing me the dispatch case in which he carried his drawing materials. He gave me his fife, too. Then he kicked off his boots, skinned out of his trousers, and peeled off his shirt.

"You don't mean to go back there?" I cried.

"There are two or three wounded men on the other side," he explained. "Somebody's got to help them."

I sighed and started unbuttoning my tunic, but Julian waved me back.

"Stay here and tend Will," Julian insisted.

Will Scott, pale as death, managed to grab my wrist and keep me there. Julian splashed into the stream and swam across. I counted two other trips he made, and I have to say it was close to the bravest thing I ever saw.

"Just goes to show," Will mumbled. "Don't have to be tall to have grit."

I nodded. Will was slowly bleeding to death, and there wasn't a thing I could do about it.

"You did fair yourself," I told him. "Mr. Lincoln knew what he was doing, giving you another chance."

"He just let the rebs do the generals' work for them," Will said, wheezing and spitting blood out of the corner of his mouth. "But I suppose my folks will take it easier this way."

I tried to stop shaking. It was hard, sitting there among the dying. Lando was gone. A few feet away Jerry Bishop and his pa sat, both of them bleeding. Who knew how many other Company D friends were among the dead? And I was haunted by the thought that any minute some reb might drop Julian, and I would be shy another friend.

"It's time to retire, boys," Captain Harrington announced. "Help the wounded. Stretcher-bearers, bring along the serious cases."

I gazed up at him. Stretcher-bearers? Where were the stretchers?

"Never mind," Julian said, grabbing my shoulder with his soggy hand as I angrily turned toward the captain. "Help me with Will."

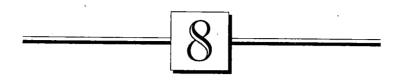

WE CALLED IT the Battle of Lee's Mills or Burnt Chimneys, after the ruins of an old mill near the rebel line. The rebs themselves called it the Dam Number One skirmish.

"It was no skirmish, though," a captured reb grumbled. "It was more of a dam battle."

It was to me anyway. When the smoke had cleared, and the companies reassembled, I realized how costly our attack had been. Company D alone lost eight men killed and another mortally wounded. Many more were wounded. The regiment proper counted twenty-six dead and over sixty wounded. Nine of those died within the next week or so.

We musicians spent that week helping Doc Jones tend the sick and wounded. It was the worst sort of job. Between the heat and the flies, those poor fellows suffered terribly. About all a boy could do to help was mop their foreheads with a cool cloth, bring them a cool drink of water, or write a last letter home.

Will Scott was one of the first to die. He was alert a good bit of the time, but the pain got a lot worse, and his eyes lost their focus. Julian scribbled a last few words to send Will's family. Then Doc Jones told us to cover him up.

"His suffering is over," the doctor said, sighing. "Nobody will ever fault that young man for anything again."

I nodded my agreement. Then I walked off into the nearby trees and wrote a letter of my own. I managed to compose a few ordinary lines to Ma, assuring her I was still whole and being well looked after, and I greeted James and Charley. Then, without really intending it, I told them of the battle. I wrote about the gore and the blood and the moans of the dying. When I finished, I stared at the words and noticed my paper was spotted with water droplets. I was crying.

Two powerful hands seized my shoulders and squeezed them tightly.

"Pa?" I gasped, looking up into his sorrowful eyes.

"Mind if I have a glance?" he asked, nodding toward the letter.

"No," I said, passing it to him. He sat beside me, and I settled in under his arm the way I had when I was a child. He read the words with some effort. My penmanship was barely adequate at the best of times, and the tears had caused the marks made by my pencil to stray here and there.

"I didn't intend to say so much about the fighting," I confessed when Pa returned the letter.

"You could send just the first part, son," he noted. "She might take alarm to read the rest."

"Yes, sir," I agreed. I carefully tore the paper, and he smiled his approval.

"You've seen the elephant now, Willie," he observed, choosing the phrase veteran soldiers were fond of using to signify a man's first time under fire. "What did you think of it?"

"Not much," I said, frowning.

"I understand the regiment lost a hundred men. There's talk of sending someone back to Saint Jay to recruit. You could speak to Colonel Hyde about it."

"I guess I'll stay," I told Pa. "I feel like I'm doing something here. Maybe not much, but more than I would accomplish back home."

"You've done a good deal already," Pa argued. "Your lieutenant speaks highly of you, and Dr. Jones praises your work. It was the doc who arranged for me to visit."

"He gives us stick candy, too," I muttered. "Looks after the children. Pa, I don't feel much like a child anymore."

"I believe you have some time left before you'll be borrowing my razor."

"Lando couldn't boast much of a mustache, Pa, but he's just as dead as anybody. I don't suppose age matters so much."

"No, you're right about that, son," Pa agreed. "This army buries plenty of boys. I wouldn't like to think you could be one of them."

"Don't worry," I said, sighing. "I won't take any chances."

"No?" he asked, probing my eyes with his own. "I spoke with the Bishops. Jerry said you dashed about like a rabbit, drawing shots like a flower draws bees."

"There were some who splashed back and forth across the stream, rescuing helpless soldiers," I argued, thinking of Julian in particular. "Me, I just sat and tended the wounded. I shot no rebels. I'm not a real soldier, Pa. Just a drummer."

That notion haunted me as I went about my nursing duties. I was really no better than a spectator, close enough to see and hear, but not truly a member of the fraternity of soldiers. You had to carry and fire a rifle to be admitted to that select group.

I was out gathering firewood the last day of April when a rock nicked my shoulder.

"Willie?" an odd voice called.

"Who's there?" I asked, dropping my bundle of kindling and gazing warily around at the dense underbrush.

"Shhhh," the voice pleaded. "It's Jeb."

He stepped out from behind a nearby tree, and I scowled. His grin faded as he followed my gaze to the sling holding his left arm.

"Ain't much," he assured me. "No more'n a crease. You Vermont boys let loose a volley or two at us, and I got nicked."

"I don't know that I can go on trading, not with the war on," I declared. "I've had friends killed."

"I've buried a brother," he growled. "Still, it seems like the old truce is on between the lines, and my sergeant's got a thirst for Yank coffee."

I tried to harden my eyes, but when he took off his cap and grinned, I couldn't help laughing.

"You've still got your ears, eh?" I asked.

"Poor shots, you Yanks," he observed. "I did my best to shy from range, of course. Still, a good shot . . ."

"I'll get some coffee," I told him.

"Here," he said, dragging a basket out from behind the tree. It contained vegetables and tobacco.

"How much—" I began.

"No dickerin', Willie," he said, frowning. "Just give us what yuh figure's fair. I trust yuh."

"It just doesn't seem possible for us to be at war," I cried, sitting on a nearby rock. "There's not a good enough reason. Jeb, I've been madder at neighbors."

"Don't yuh go tryin' to figure out weighty matters now," he scolded. "That's not for drummers to do. All we can do is follow our orders and maybe cheer the men some. Do their swappin' for 'em. It's hard enough dodgin' musket balls and sergeants."

"I guess," I confessed. "You keep your head down, Jeb. I'll bring your coffee tomorrow."

"Best do it tonight," he urged. I thought to ask why, but I didn't. He could no more speak of his regiment's orders than I could.

Three days after we completed the trade, the rebel guns across the stream opened up a fierce bombardment. That night burning fuses etched arcs across the blackened sky, and I cowered in my tent, praying the rebs were aiming at some other, more important target.

We soon learned the reason for the bombardment. On Sunday, May 4, word reached us that the rebels had abandoned Yorktown. All those fireworks were just a cover for the reb retreat. Like the other regiments of the Army of the Potomac, we packed up our camp and began marching toward Richmond.

"Three cheers for General McClellan!" someone shouted as the army commander rode by with his staff.

We Vermonters tossed our caps and howled for the general.

"Boys, we have to press the rebel!" the general demanded. "Pursue. Punish him!"

We were eager to do just that, but the chase was never more than halfhearted. Colonel Hyde had us assembled and ready to move, but we were ordered over and over again to wait. Lieutenant Buck muttered a curse or two, and General Smith expressed his dismay over the delay.

Finally, orders or not, the colonel instructed us to occupy the rebel trenches.

We formed columns and warily approached the silent rebel line. The trenches were empty, though. A short distance back, several tents remained, as did many makeshift mud and log shelters. I discovered a message carved into the door of one hut.

WELKOM TO RATSVIL
ALL THE SKEETERS YU WANT
INJOY DEM

The author had carved a figure just below with over-sized ears. The letters JD stood prominently on the fig-ure's chest.

"Jeb," I muttered.

"I'm halfway glad that those rebs still have a sense of humor," Cal remarked as he grabbed my arm and hur-ried me back into line. "They may need it."

"We could all use a laugh or two these days," Russ added. "We're still a long way from Richmond."

As if we didn't have enough troubles, May greeted us with worse weather. The days were gray, bleak, and cold. We marched through one downpour after another, and the roads only got worse.

"Virginia's left the Union, all right," Cal observed. "Now she's in the mud."

The Vermont Brigade, as General Brooks's regiments had come to be called, cautiously followed the fleeing rebels to the pretty little town of Williamsburg. There we took up position in a narrow field between two creeks. Across the way a series of imposing rebel forts frowned down at us.

"They can't mean to attack that!" I heard Captain

Harrington object one night as I prepared to call the company to its nightly dress parade.

"I am beginning to wonder if this army means to attack anything," Colonel Hyde replied. "We lose more men to fevers than ten rebel regiments could kill."

One morning a whole pack of riders appeared in camp a few minutes after reveille.

"Attention!" Sergeant Currier barked.

"Finally," Cal said. "Orders."

"At ease," Captain Harrington muttered. "There's not a general among them."

In fact, they were war correspondents visiting the field. They talked with us, asked questions, and passed on news of the war.

"The big news is that Norfolk has fallen," a youngish fellow from Boston explained. "President Lincoln led a few companies of soldiers into the city himself, and all the defenders were gone. It was an easy capture."

"What about the *Merrimack?*" Russ asked.

"Blew herself up," a second correspondent told us. "The rebs burned what remained of the navy yard, but we did capture some supplies and a quantity of cotton. Now that we control both banks of the James River, we can send the fleet up to Richmond and secure the city's surrender."

"Then the war will be over soon," Cal said, wiping his forehead. "The rebs won't have any stomach for a fight once Richmond falls."

"I don't believe it will be that easy," the Bostonian said, shaking his head. "Ships alone may not thwart Joe Johnston. General McClellan believes the rebels have a hundred thousand men in their trenches, and more are arriving daily. Soon we may be on the defensive ourselves."

I glanced around at my companions. It was not welcome news. There we were, halfway up the Peninsula, and this fellow was saying we might have to fight our way back down.

I don't know where the correspondents attained their news, but the rebs facing us outside of Williamsburg were ragged scarecrows with ranks far thinner than our own. At every turn we drove them toward their capital, and as the final days of May dawned, we were so close to Richmond that we could keep time by the sound of the city's church bells.

"It won't be long, son," Pa told me. "They can't hope to stop us now."

That next morning, after beating reveille, I was surprised to discover Colonel Hyde standing outside my tent.

"Drummer Johnston, we have a problem," he said, frowning at me.

"We do, sir?" I asked. "Or I do?"

"We do," the colonel said, betraying a trace of a smile. "You have served with this regiment since December, but it appears that you were never officially mustered."

"I signed the book," I protested.

"I have no doubt as to your intentions, sir, but the fact remains that you have drawn no pay."

"Pay, sir?" I asked. "You don't pay drummers. I'm not a real soldier, after all."

"Musicians in my regiment are allotted a full private's pay," the colonel insisted. "Thirteen dollars a month. Dating back to December, that totals sixty-five dollars. Now, if that sounds agreeable, repeat after me the official oath and sign the enlistment forms."

I did just that. Then I eagerly waited for Colonel Hyde to hand me my sixty-five dollars. The colonel noted my open hand and laughed.

"I am afraid a soldier's pay can be slow in coming," he said. "Some of the men were paid back in November, I believe. New recruits have to be patient."

"New?" I asked.

"You have only been a soldier a few minutes, Willie," he noted. "Give or take six months."

"I suppose it could be worse," I observed. "They might not feed us but every six months, too. Not that they overdo it any," I added, noting my shrinking middle.

"I suppose you should immediately report to Dr. Jones then," the colonel declared, tapping my shoulder. "For a candy ration."

I couldn't locate the doc, but it wasn't very important. I didn't even care too much about the money. There wasn't anything to spend it on out there in the Virginia mud. I felt a little taller, signing those papers. And knowing that I was worth thirteen dollars a month to somebody made me value myself.

I didn't stand around congratulating myself for very long. That evening a tremendous thunderstorm boiled up overhead, drenching every inch of us. I saw cavalry horses stuck in mud up to their knees. Company F's drummer, not much bigger than me, was close to sucked under by that mud. When his tentmates hoisted him out, he was bare below the waist. That bog had stripped his pants, drawers, and boots!

"Better him than me," Julian told me as we cowered under the hospital tent awning.

"Poor fellow," I replied. "He's got to try and wrangle more clothes out of the quartermaster!"

A tremendous bolt of lightning struck nearby, shaking the ground.

"That is hell's artillery, boys," Colonel Hyde told us.

"Old soldiers believe it means there's a battle coming," Sergeant Currier said as he shooed Julian and me out from our refuge. "If that's the case, we'll need musicians who can stay awake tomorrow. Get some rest!"

I suppose the sergeant thought I could sleep under a blanket on that muddy hillside! I tried, but I passed most of that night shivering beside my tentmates under one of the quartermaster wagons.

The thunderstorm turned out to be the omen Sergeant Currier suspected. On the last day of May the rebs attacked near a place called Fair Oaks. I could hear the cannons echoing through the hills to my left, but we were too far away to catch a glimpse of the actual fighting. It was no skirmish, though. Each side lost more than five thousand men!

"The rebs tried to break our line, but they were thrown back with severe losses," Colonel Hyde told us at dress parade. "The road to Richmond is open, and we will soon be parading through the rebel capital itself!"

We cheered the notion and tossed our hats. We were close to victory, and we knew it.

"Look there," Russ shouted, pointing his hand at the far horizon. It was the first clear afternoon in days, and we could actually sees the spires of the city. Richmond! We were almost there.

"Soon, boys," the colonel assured us. "Soon."

9

SUMMER DAYS IN VIRGINIA stretch themselves, and as the weather improved, we learned to look back on the cooler days of May with a degree of fondness. The Army of the Potomac was settling in on the outskirts of Richmond, but the generals didn't seem in any great hurry to push the rebels into a fight. Rumors of all sorts spread through our company. Some said the rebel president, Jefferson Davis, was packing up the government and heading south. The new rebel commander, a fellow named Robert E. Lee, was considered by most to be too old and tired to offer us much resistance. After all, General McClellan had already chased Lee around the mountains of West Virginia the year before.

I myself saw no evidence of rebs heading anywhere. They were improving their lines, and our pickets fired at their scouts. Rebel cavalry was probing our flanks, and from time to time a few of their guns would fire into our lines. Meanwhile, up in the Shenandoah Valley, Stonewall Jackson thrashed two different Union armies, and there was a rumor Jackson had now come to Richmond, bringing fifty thousand veterans with him. Old Stonewall seemed to pop up on the left, on the right, in the center, and even at Yorktown!

The Third Vermont passed the middle part of June

building a bridge over a putrid quagmire called the Chickahominy River. It wasn't much of a stream, but no wagon could get across.

"It is absolutely vital to the campaign's success that we build this bridge," Captain Harrington explained. "To avoid attacking Richmond frontally, General McClellan intends to move half the army across the river and come in behind the rebel flanks."

I suppose on paper it must have made good sense, but all that country was a maze of thick woods, swamps, and streams. Sometimes you could barely walk through there single file. It was just about perfect for ambushing an enemy. Every single time our company stood guard or served as pickets, I was sure the rebs would charge out of those trees and take the whole batch of us prisoner.

Bridge building was no improvement over picket or guard duty. Fortunately I wasn't overworked myself. Most of the time I carried nail buckets or brought tools out from the quartermaster. Cal, Moses, and Russ labored particularly hard erecting the pilings, and whenever they left the river, their legs would be covered with big, fat, bloodsucking leeches.

"It's just a new kind of reb cavalry," Russ told me when I helped pluck the infernal creatures from his thighs. "We'll have the last laugh when we parade through Richmond."

I wasn't so sure about that, though. Stories of rebels raiding our depots miles behind the lines sent shivers up my spine.

"That's all over with now," Julian told me one morning when we washed our clothes in a tub at the edge of camp. "Jeb Stuart, the rebel cavalry general, took a few thousand men all the way around the army. They burned some wagons and looted some supplies, but it was mostly a nuisance."

"How do you know?" I asked.

"I spent yesterday at headquarters, carrying messages for Colonel Hyde," he explained. "Don't you worry, Willie. The generals know what they're doing."

My tentmates and I were far from certain of that. Some soldiers in General Fitz John Porter's corps captured a handful of rebel deserters. It turned out they were from Stonewall Jackson's army.

"See there?" I told Julian the next day. "Trouble is sure to follow."

"Oh, you know how rebels boast," he replied. "They were probably pickets who got tired of keeping watch and decided to come over to our lines. Stonewall Jackson? He's supposed to be up near Harper's Ferry."

"From what I've heard, he just about never is where he's supposed to be."

"Kind of like you, eh?" Sergeant Currier barked.

I turned, stiffened, and waited for the sergeant to give me a chewing out. He only waved me back to the company, and I hurried along.

Those June days I judge the Army of the Potomac had a hundred thousand generals. Every man in the army had his own notion of what we should do. I myself didn't care as long as it was something. Since completing the bridge, we had far too little to do. The men were getting anxious, and we drummers and fifers passed most afternoons playing cards or tormenting our elders. I also saw Pa a time or two. Everything changed the final week of June.

As I recall, it was a fine Wednesday morning, the twenty-fifth, when General McClellan finally decided to probe the enemy defenses. Every regiment in the army formed up and took position, but only a few companies were actually sent forward. It was like Lee's Mills all over again except it wasn't the Third Vermont that got shot up this time, and we lost close to five hundred men.

The galling thing for me was that we couldn't even hear the shooting. Nobody did anything out our way.

"Don't be in such a hurry to see your second fight, Willie," Russ scolded me when I complained about addled generals. "Before the last one I had two big brothers. Now there's just Blackie, and he's none too well."

I thought about it a moment, and it tore at me some, recalling Lando's bloody chest. Waiting was almost as bad, though. It just seemed to me it was better to go ahead and get the fighting over.

That night the whole army was restless, and no one slept particularly well. Captain Harrington ordered me to spread my blankets outside his tent.

"If the rebels decide to attack us by night, I want you at hand, Johnston," he explained. "You can beat out assembly and rouse the men."

If a few thousand rebs started charging through the camp, I don't think a single drum would have made much of a difference. Nevertheless the jittery captain roused me a dozen times.

"What's that?" he asked the first time. "Did you hear something?" he cried later.

In truth, it reminded me of looking after Charley on a stormy night. Of course, Charley was just five years old.

It turned out that Captain Harrington's worries weren't completely unfounded. That next morning the wind carried sounds of firing. The rebs attacked General Porter's corps and fought them most of the day. Colonel

Hyde formed our regiment, and we marched around some, but we never did get into battle.

On Friday messengers arrived with word that fighting had resumed. Porter and his men had repelled the rebs the day before. Now General McClellan had ordered a retreat. General Brooks rode by, waving his hat and encouraging our efforts, and you could feel the blood starting to pump. We cheered him wildly, and afterward we formed up by companies and sent skirmishers out in front. Once again the fighting took place elsewhere. The brigade was shifted from place to place, and we finished the afternoon digging up dirt and forming earthworks behind a nasty little stream.

About the only good we did was to help some of the worn-out stragglers from Porter's corps. We musicians were detailed to help load ambulances with wounded, so Julian and I assisted a few men into the backs of quartermaster wagons sent out by the regimental doctors. We carried them to a small depot called Savage's Station. Then we returned to the Third.

I passed that night with the rest of Company D, sleeping in our makeshift trench at the edge of the stream. The mosquitoes attacked us mercilessly, and the wind carried odors of scorched logs, gunpowder, and something else—a new and overpowering foul smell of blood and death.

"Willie, you asleep?" Russ asked around midnight.

"Not yet," I told him. "It's hard to get comfortable."

"Look over there," he said, pointing to a hundred flickering pinpricks of light across the swamp. "Reb campfires," he explained. "Tomorrow they'll be coming at us."

"You think so?" I asked nervously.

"We've been lucky so far," he said, sighing. "Just poor Lando. Who do you suppose will be next?"

"I try not to think," I said, trembling. "Hope it's not me. At least not yet. I have a birthday next month, you know. I'll be twelve."

"Sometimes I could swear you're fifty, Willie."

"I confess this war's aged me some."

"It's turned us all old," Russ observed. "I guess it's feeling death's breath."

"What?"

"My grandma explained it that way, Willie. She said sometimes death is so close you can feel its breath on your neck. That's just how I feel. Half of me wants to cry and the rest wants to scream!"

"Yes," I agreed. "It doesn't seem at all fair."

"You scared?"

"Sometimes," I admitted, trying to catch a glimpse of his face in the faint moonlight. "I worry that I'll run away, that I won't do what I'm supposed to, and that you or Cal or somebody will get shot because of it."

"You'll do fine," Russ assured me. "Better than the captain, I'd bet."

"He was none too steady at Lee's Mills, but I don't think he plans to hang back this time," I said. "He knows some of the men are whispering, and I hear Sam Pingree went home and talked about who crossed the creek and who didn't."

"I wish I hadn't. Wish Lando hadn't, either."

"More will get killed."

"I know," Russ confessed. "They say Porter lost five thousand yesterday."

"Five thousand?"

"And it's not over, Willie. Not by half."

I never did find any rest that night, but I did close my eyes for a time. Half an hour later Captain Harrington shook me awake.

"Beat assembly," he whispered. "We're withdrawing."

I did as ordered, and as the sound of my lone drum echoed across the land, bugles and other drums responded. Across the swamp, reb pickets appeared, and one or two of them exchanged shots with us. Nobody appeared in a hurry to start a fight in that nest of briers and mud, though. We formed lines and withdrew by company. It seemed as if the entire Army of the Potomac was on the march. Only this time, we were not advancing on Richmond. No, now we were heading away, toward the James River and the safety of the fleet.

That morning I saw General Smith for the first time since the fighting had begun. He was standing under a tall tree, writing out dispatches. Not far away General William Franklin, commander of the Sixth Corps, was doing likewise. It seemed odd, seeing generals out on hillsides. Usually they had forests of tents around them, or they located their headquarters in houses.

"Now they're no better off than you and me, Willie," Cal observed. "Some Pennsylvania fellows said there are headquarters tents and papers burning from here to the James. Seems like Porter's regiments lost most of their blankets and all their tents."

For once, I was thankful the quartermasters had hauled our equipment to the rear. But as fast as we were retreating, I couldn't be certain the wagons were staying ahead of the rebels.

For the first time that Saturday, the Third Vermont occupied a position of importance. General Franklin deployed the Sixth Corps along the edge of a small farm and atop a low ridge shielding Savage's Station.

"Boys, we're in a real pickle," General Smith said, speaking to each regiment up and down the line. "Behind us is the supply train for half the army. Food, ammunition, medical supplies. The division hospital is back there with hundreds of General Porter's soldiers, many of them badly wounded. I cannot abide the thought of abandoning those brave comrades to the enemy. Will you fight to prevent their capture?"

"Yes, sir!" we howled.

"I knew you would," he replied. "Vermonters have iron in their backbones. They won't flee at the first shot. We have a duty ahead of us, boys, and we'll do it, by God."

As the general departed, a new spirit surged through our ranks. Each soldier checked his cartridges, and some sharpened their bayonets. No one had shaved in days, and those capable of growing chin whiskers took on a strangely sinister appearance. We must have appeared like a band of cutthroats. Well, maybe not me, but older fellows like Cal.

That day we had our first truly good look at the enemy. Before, at Lee's Mills, they had hidden behind their earthworks or cowered behind trees. Now they marched out in front of us on the Williamsburg Road, flags flying, with their drums beating and bugles blaring.

"Form line!" Sergeant Currier barked, and I beat out the command. To our right and left the other Vermont regiments marched forward. The Fifth Vermont, which had failed to advance to our aid at Lee's Mills, now led the advance. Before us I recognized a Louisiana flag.

Their banners identified them as the Fifth Louisiana. The Fifth Vermont charged directly at them.

We, too, advanced, but it was our brother regiment that received most of the attention. The Louisianans leveled their muskets and fired in ranks. One volley, two volleys, three volleys staggered the Fifth Vermont. I gazed in horror as whole handfuls of men fell. A withering fire rose from the woods to their left, too, and the Fifth simply disintegrated. Those able to fell back. Others lay where they had fallen. Over two hundred of them failed to stir.

"Fire!" Lieutenant Buck shouted, and Company D halted, leveled their rifles, and fired. The rebels replied with a sharp volley. We were both at extreme range, and only a few men on either side were hit. I glanced around for Captain Harrington, but the dust kicked up by our feet choked the air and obscured my vision. I heard his voice call for a second volley. Then the din of rifles deafened me.

A brigade messenger rode over, shouting, "Withdraw. Reform."

I glanced around for someone in authority. Lieutenant Buck nodded to me.

"Beat the retreat, Willie," he said sadly. "The others have been driven back, and our flanks are exposed."

It was true. On the left, where the Fifth had made its charge, a few wounded tried to drag themselves to safety. On the right we were equally naked. Slowly we fell back, warily eyeing the Louisianans. They paused, allowing our escape.

The Battle of Savage's Station, as it became known, was over. The consequences were not. The Third formed a new line to shield the hospital, but riders arrived ordering us to withdraw.

"You can't mean to abandon all those soldiers!" Lieutenant Buck shouted. "There are only a few rebel regiments coming, and they are in no real hurry. We can hold them off."

"Don't yell at me," the messenger countered. "These orders come straight from General McClellan. He's worried the rebs are working around behind us. Better to give up a few wounded than lose the whole army."

Most of us didn't see it that way. I didn't have a lot of experience fighting wars, but I knew it was a cowardly thing to leave your wounded behind. There were hundreds of them, too.

"Willie, you think you can help some?" Lieutenant Buck asked.

"I think so," I answered, nervously pulling out my bandage bag.

"Do what you can, son," he suggested. "You have some time. Just don't get caught here when we leave. Understand?"

"Yes, sir," I replied.

Most of the regimental musicians headed over to help the doctors. We did our best to bandage the walking wounded so that they might escape with the rest of the army. We loaded a few men into an empty wagon, but a major walked over and shook his head.

"There is a tangle of wagons a mile and a half long up ahead," he explained. "We're burning every wagon left, to keep them out of rebel hands. I can't even be sure I can get the horses through."

"Sorry," I said as I helped a one-armed sixteen-year-old out of the wagon.

"You did what you could," he told me.

We were able to give each of the wounded an extra

blanket. The quartermasters were doling out blankets, shoes, and all sorts of food. I split a can of peaches with Julian Scott, and each of us acquired a new pair of boots. What remained was set alight. It pained me, seeing all those supplies turning into ugly gray smoke. But I knew the generals were determined not to give the rebels a greater victory than they had earned.

We did our best to make the wounded soldiers comfortable. It was hard. They knew the grim chance of surviving their wounds. When they were prisoners, the odds could only grow worse. I tried to avoid their helpless gazes. Ghostly eyes peered out of bloody bandages, and legless cripples stared bitterly as we prepared to march away. Behind the hospital rose a mound of amputated arms and legs, and beyond that the long rows of blanket-covered corpses.

"It's time," Lieutenant Buck called, pointing to an approaching line of rebels. I grabbed my drum and raced to take my place at the head of our column. The advancing rebs began to shout, and I took out my sticks and began beating the drum. I hit it harder and harder. It was as if all the fear and sorrow of a hundred wars flowed into my fingers.

"Willie, you'll have need of that drum," Cal said, clamping his hands onto my arms. "Beat it a hair softer."

I glanced up at him and frowned. He nodded, and I resumed my drumming. I could hear the regiment's other drummers likewise softening their beat. We now hoped only to muffle the moans of the wounded and the pounding of our hearts. Only that.

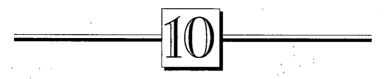

THE THIRD VERMONT left Savage's Station with heavy hearts. We hated the notion of abandoning our helpless comrades. It galled us to see our army scrambling away like a bunch of scared rabbits.

"We're running like rats from a sinking ship," Cal muttered.

That wasn't far from the mark. We trudged southward better than an hour before reaching a stagnant creek known as White Oak Swamp. General Smith had taken on the task of forming a rear guard with his division, and the Vermont Brigade was ordered to cross the swamp, dismantle a rickety bridge, and hold any pursuing rebels at bay while the rest of the army made its escape to the James River.

I never imagined that anything on earth could transform our proud army into the disorganized rabble I witnessed on that retreat. Soldiers straggled from their regiments and wandered about, dazed and confused. I saw officers cowering behind trees. One major formed his men into a line and ordered them to destroy their rifles one by one.

"They can move faster without their equipment," he told Lieutenant Buck.

I didn't see what use an unarmed soldier could be.

Later on, we retrieved twenty or thirty discarded rifles strewn along the muddy road beyond the swamp.

"Better to smash a rifle than give it over to the rebs," Cal observed as we destroyed the weapons.

Once the last company of the brigade's trailing regiment crossed the bridge, General Brooks issued orders positioning us along the swamp. The Third held the bridge itself, and most of us devoted our time to erecting a makeshift wall a few feet behind the stream. Using their bayonets, the soldiers dug up mud and formed it into mounds. In this way they made a short wall, but the other side was scooped out like a trench. We ended up with rifle pits four feet deep. They were just about perfect for shooting attacking rebels from cover.

Sergeant Currier took a dozen men and began tearing down the bridge. It didn't look like much, but the engineers had done a better job than I thought. It required two hours to destroy the supports, and finally General Brooks sent over some powder. We then blew the bridge apart.

The rebels took their time catching up to us. I guess they had been slowed by the field hospital and the hundreds of wounded they had to guard. At any rate the enemy approached the swamp cautiously. They didn't repeat our Lee's Mills mistake. Instead of charging our lines, they held back and opened up a cannonade.

I later learned there were twenty-five thousand Union troops lined up along the swamp that day. Parts of the Second and the Fourth Corps had turned back to support General Franklin's Sixth. Our guns answered the rebel cannons, and a bit later the enemy batteries grew quiet. We raised a cheer for our gunners, but the battle had not properly begun. At a nearby farm, soldiers dressed in gray and blue surged across open fields only to be thrown back to their trenches. Each side lost close to four thousand men that day. The Third Vermont held its ground and punished the enemy. Company D was lucky. The rebs never pressed their attack along our stretch of the creek, and we had no casualties. The rebs shot at us from time to time, but their aim proved poor.

We greeted dusk confidently. The sounds of gunfire farther west echoed through the hollows, but the rebels opposite our line kept quiet. In truth, I didn't think anyone could get across that swamp and dislodge us. The quartermaster distributed some dried beef and a few loaves of bread. I gobbled mine greedily and glanced around, hoping there might be a little more.

"I wish we had thought to grab some food before they burned those supply wagons," Russ grumbled. "We'll not be seeing any breakfast, I'll bet."

"Didn't you have enough to carry?" Cal asked.

"Nobody ever promised you a full belly, did they?" Lieutenant Buck added.

"Actually, Captain Harrington did," I replied. "But I suppose we're better off than the wounded."

Everyone frowned when I reminded them of the abandoned hospital, and I was sorry for speaking of it. Lieutenant Buck did locate an extra loaf of bread, though, and we fuzzies shared our portion.

Sergeant Currier assembled us in the trench and assigned night watches. After posting pickets, he urged the rest of us to get some rest.

"Tomorrow may be another long day," he warned.

We all nodded and began searching for a dry spot to lie down. I piled some leaves onto the ground and rolled out my blankets. Then I noticed the sergeant.

"Are you holding up, youngster?" he asked me.

"Yes, sergeant," I replied. "A little scared maybe, but nobody's shot me yet."

"Well, you're a small target," he observed.

"I try to be," I admitted. "Doesn't seem much of an advantage to be big just now."

"This where you plan to sleep?"

"Unless it starts raining or the rebel guns open up."

"Well, we'll all be in the trenches then anyway," he told me. "I'll just tie this kerchief in the branches here, over your head."

"Why?" I asked.

"We might get marching orders before the sun rises again," he explained. "I need to know where you are. You may have to rouse the men."

I nodded somberly. I judged a sound night's sleep might be hard to come by. It was.

I faded off as soon as I closed my eyes, but my dreams were troubled. I saw Lando lying dead at my feet, but this time his brothers Blackie and Russ were beside him. I saw a hundred rebs chase after me with sharpened bayonets. I turned around, searching for help, but I was alone. I felt the cold steel pierce my insides, and I screamed myself awake.

"Calm down, son," Sergeant Currier said, clamping his hands onto my shoulders. "Didn't mean to startle you so."

"What?" I cried.

"We have our orders. It's time to rouse the men." I scrambled around, searching for my drum, but he stopped me. "Do it quietly," the sergeant advised. "No need to tip our hand to the rebs."

I went among the men, warily waking them. I could

100

tell that I wasn't the only one who was troubled by nightmares. Russ leaped to his feet and grabbed his rifle. Fortunately it wasn't loaded.

We quietly packed our gear, and I was amazed at how quickly the entire company assembled. Captain Harrington, who had seemingly disappeared most of the day, addressed us in a whisper.

"We have been ordered back again," he explained. "The whole army is making a stand at Malvern Hill, a few miles closer to the James. General Brooks is pulling regiments out one at a time. It's our turn. Keep quiet and don't attract attention. It wouldn't do to have the rebs charging into gaps in our lines."

Once again we were pulling up stakes and retreating. It seemed somehow shameful. We were in as strong a position as I could imagine, and from what some of the stragglers from Porter's corps said, the rebs had yet to penetrate a single one of our positions. What was worse, our midnight skedaddle was a hopeless rout. Companies and even regiments got lost in the dark. Whole units went off on side roads and became tangled in the dense underbrush. Weary men threw away their bedding, canteens, even cartridge boxes and rifles. Sadly, I saw three abandoned drums.

"You might as well toss yours over there, too, Willie," Cal advised. "You won't need it tonight. Truth is, the way this army fights, all you need is a good pair of boots."

I frowned. Cal had a point. And as we trudged along, that drum seemed to grow heavier every mile. I had a hard time keeping up.

"Leave that fool drum," my friends urged.

I couldn't, though. What use was a drummer without a drum?

For once I wished it was raining. Thousands of tramping feet had turned the road into a cloud of choking dust. Every inch of me was coated with the chalky powder! I followed the example of my companions and stepped out of line. I shed my pack and stripped off my tunic. After tying it onto my rucksack, I opened up my shirt so that the bare flesh of my chest could catch the hint of breeze that survived the stifling Virginia morning. Then I slung the rucksack over one shoulder and my drum sash over the other.

"Mind some company?" Pa called from a few feet away. I could barely make out his tired face in the faint predawn light, but it cheered me nevertheless.

"Still two Johnstons in the Third, eh?" I asked.

"No holes in you, either, then?" he countered. I managed half a laugh, and he clasped my hands. "Your ma was right, Willie. You should have stayed home," he added as he took my rucksack and slung it over his shoulder. "There, it's some easier now, isn't it?"

"Yes, sir," I agreed.

"We had better catch up with the regiment," Pa said, urging me back onto the road. "It's no particular joy fighting with the Third, but it's considerably better than finding yourself with one of these other outfits."

I'm not entirely certain how long we walked that eerie morning, but when the sun finally rose, we were creeping up onto Malvern Hill. It really wasn't a hill in the sense I was used to. It was more a gradual rise. The only good road to the James River crossed that rise, though, and the sole other way to Harrison's Landing, where the generals had decided to make our final stand, was through a wilderness of swamps and thick woods.

Individual soldiers stumbled along the hill, searching

for familiar faces. The generals had ordered the regimental colors displayed, and I located the Third by its battle flag. Otherwise, one regiment pretty much resembled the next. No one was in correct uniform. Some of the men had left half their clothes behind. I retrieved my rucksack from Pa, but my tunic had fallen out, and my shirt was torn and tattered by briers. I had a bad tear in my trousers, too, but at least I had them. I spied an artillery battery with three men wrapped in their blankets.

Close to three-fourths of the army assembled at Malvern Hill, and I wager there were a hundred cannons frowning out from our positions. General McClellan put in an appearance, and regiment by regiment we cheered him. Then he conferred with the other generals and rode off to Harrison's Landing.

"It's said he passed the night in a gunboat," Cal whispered. "I don't suppose there's much fear he'll get shot."

"Generals are pitiful little use any time," Sergeant Currier said, grinning. "Up here in the front line they really get in the way."

I couldn't help laughing, even when Lieutenant Buck glanced over.

"There's truth to it, lieutenant," Cal insisted.

"You weren't always an officer," Currier added. "You once had some sense yourself."

I feared the lieutenant might explode, but he only laughed.

"You can't argue with the truth," he said.

The rebels marched up later. It was a marvelous sight, all those neat lines and precise formations. When we had fought before, it had been man to man, in trenches, behind trees, tangled in swamp and woods. The enemy that came out to challenge us now seemed more deadly and fearsome than ever. But although their attack began well, most of their advances were halfhearted. Some rebel regiments had already suffered terrible casualties.

At Malvern Hill, the Third was spared the brunt of the fighting, and from what I could see, we were truly blessed. The charging rebel regiments were torn to pieces by our guns or cut down like rows of wheat before a scythe. It was both inspiring and horrible at the same time. Confederate cannons and riflery took a toll on our army as well. When the rebels finally gave up the attack, six thousand of them had fallen. Three thousand loyal Union men also fell, and absolutely nothing was accomplished.

"We ought to cheer them," Cal suggested as the rebel regiments retired.

"No," Sergeant Currier argued. "We're not through fighting them yet. When they lay down their arms and give up this rebellion, I'll cheer every one of them. Not before."

I would have hollered and thrown my hat anyway, but I wasn't certain I had the strength. Most of us collapsed where we stood and tried to rest some.

The order to retreat arrived early that next morning. Most of us were hungry and exhausted. Some cold beef and biscuits had been distributed, but I still had most of mine. I had been too tired to chew. I tapped out assembly, and Company D roused itself. The slopes of Malvern Hill were littered with bodies, and many of them were moving. Squads of our soldiers set out to tend the wounded and retrieve any capable of surviving. It was an awful scene, much worse when the mist cleared and we could see the thousands of shattered bodies.

I found myself stumbling along the line. I saw Julian Scott sitting beside a cannon, sketching the awful spectacle.

"We should go down there and help," I told him.

"Willie, you can hardly walk," he said, shaking his head. "Look at your leg! You need some doctoring yourself."

I noticed an ugly tear in my left leg below the knee. Something sharp had opened a considerable gash, and blood was trickling through the dust and grime.

"Sit down a minute," Julian urged. "I'll do it."

He poured some water from his canteen onto the leg and wiped away most of the dirt. He then dressed the wound.

"Thanks," I said, forcing a grin onto my face.

"Johnston!" Sergeant Currier shouted. I jumped a foot off the ground.

"Duty calls," I told Julian. I then hobbled my way to the sergeant's side and stiffened.

"Beat retreat," the sergeant growled, pointing to my drum.

"Again?" someone down the line cried. He expressed what all of us were thinking.

"Again," Sergeant Currier muttered. "Company D, form up!"

11

HARRISON'S LANDING WAS THE SITE of one of those huge Virginia manor houses that dotted the Peninsula. The plantation's fields, once white with cotton, now bloomed with row after row of conical tents. It was already a beehive of activity when the Third Vermont and the rest of General Brooks's brigade arrived. In contrast to the orderly, precisely drilled companies that had left Alexandria such a short time before, the regiment now resembled a parade of beggars. Except for a few of our officers, not a solitary man had retained all of his uniform. Most of us walked along in tatters. As soon as we arrived at the plot of ground designated as our camp, Lieutenant Buck and Sergeant Currier began barking at us to clean our weapons and button up our tunics.

"It's time you men began to look like soldiers again!" the lieutenant insisted.

"We may not altogether look the part," Cal growled, "but you go ask those rebs if we're soldiers. They'll tell you."

"If you can find the one or two we didn't shoot," Russ added.

I don't suppose we faulted the officers for yelling at us. It was their job to restore our spirits and sharpen our appearance. The trouble was that most of us no longer had enough of a uniform to pass dress parade muster. We needed food and rest more than orders.

If the sergeants and lieutenants couldn't see that, most of the colonels and generals could. Even before the quartermaster arrived with our tents, General Smith dispatched hot food to our camp.

"God bless the general," Cal declared as he chewed a pork rib. "Get me back on my feet and I'll go and discover some eggs for our breakfast!"

It was only after the provost marshals rounded up the last of the stragglers and sorted out who belonged where that we got a proper count of the regiment's casualties. A man here and there stumbled in, but Silome Persons failed to appear.

"I last saw him at Savage's Station," Cal remarked. "He was on my right during most of the fight, but later on, I don't recall seeing him there."

Nobody else remembered seeing Silome thereafter, either. He had never been talkative, and most nights you hardly knew he was in the tent. It vexed me that no one had seen him fall, and the thought that he might lie out there in the woods, wounded, haunted me. It was my obligation to tend the wounded, after all.

We fuzzies had been thinned out considerably now. Lando was dead. Blackie was at Fort Monroe, sick, and now Silome was gone, too. Horace Partlow was excused from duty with a fever, but he remained in camp. Only Cal, Russ, Moses Torrence, and myself actually assembled with the company. It was like that throughout the regiment. Companies were at half strength. Exhaustion and the intemperate climate were proving more deadly than rebel cannons.

We faced little danger from the enemy at Harrison's

Landing. A flotilla of federal gunboats anchored in the James River, and with the *Merrimack* blown up, our ships were completely fearless. Their big naval guns outranged anything the rebels could bring close to us, and even the audacious General Lee and that great rebel boogeyman, Stonewall Jackson, dared not venture near. The site was so secure, in fact, that word spread through the camp that President Lincoln had come to inspect the troops.

"He's liable to see more of some of us than others," Cal said, poking his fingers through a hole in his trousers.

"Get me some thread," I suggested. "I'll sew 'em up."

Pa kept busy patching uniforms, too, and several escaped slave women made their way around camp, offering to help sew or cook or tend the sick and wounded. Doc Jones told me they were saints among the living, those ladies. The doctor had aged twenty years, and he was wobbling around, dead on his feet.

"You ought to get some rest yourself," I told him.

"Whenever I do, somebody dies," he explained. "I can always rest later."

I was growing weary myself, and I was troubled by odd chills. Even in the midday heat, my hands would shake.

"Go see the doc," Cal advised.

The hospital had taken on the odor of death, though, and the surgeons devoted most of their time to sawing off arms and legs. I couldn't stand the smell or the hollow stares of the wounded men. I contented myself with sipping a sour tea one of the black women offered and hoping the chills would pass.

The day Mr. Lincoln came to the landing, General Smith visited our regiment.

"My old regiment," the general said, grinning. "You look sorely used, boys."

We laughed. The general joked about our tattered clothes and battered bodies.

"Tonight I'm parading the division for Mr. Lincoln, boys," he finally said. "You will try not to shame your families by appearing stark naked, won't you?"

We laughed again.

"Now, here's a drummer," he said, suddenly turning to me. "Son, what's your name?"

"Willie Johnston, Junior, sir," I replied.

"Willie, does that drum still speak?" General Smith asked.

"Good as ever," I replied.

"Let me hear it then," he said, nodding to the drum.

I drew out my sticks and beat a marching tempo.

"This retreat was hard on drums and drummers," the general said, scowling. "Do you know that I have been through a whole brigade without finding a single drum? How is it you still have yours, son?"

"I was told to hold onto 'er, sir," I answered. "A drummer isn't much use any time. Less when he's lost his drum."

"Indeed!" General Smith said, drawing me to his side and squeezing my bony shoulder. "Indeed. So here you stand, scraped and bloody, but still able to beat out your general's commands. Willie, it appears as if a singular honor has fallen upon you. When the division parades before the corps commander, General Franklin, not to mention the president himself, you will beat our sole surviving drum."

109

"Me?" I gasped.

"No one else brought his drum off the battlefield, son," the general noted.

"But I can't, sir," I argued. "There are other drummers who are older and a lot better. I lost my tunic, and my shirt's just a rag now."

"The quartermaster can supply your needs," General Smith insisted.

"He'll be hard-pressed to fit me," I said, pointing to my skinny chest and bony arms.

"Don't you worry about that, son," Pa called. "I'll see it fits."

I sighed. I tried to think of something else, but the general just laughed and clasped my hand.

"The uniform's the easy part," he whispered. "It's finding a man to wear it who deserves the honor that proves difficult. You will drum for my parade, Willie, and you will drum well. A man who does his duty in the heat of battle and confusion of retreat will have no problem performing for his president."

I was far from sure of that.

Nevertheless when the five Vermont regiments of General Brooks's brigade and the other brigades of General Smith's division assembled to pass in review before Mr. Lincoln and General Franklin, I was the solitary drummer. Fortunately the quartermaster had found a uniform, and Pa and I together did the alterations. Even better, a dozen fifers and several buglers stood with me and added their efforts to the martial music.

Julian and I stood near the center. The older fifers and buglers surrounded us, shielding us from scrutiny. Alone, I would never have been able to get my fingers to work.

When the last of the regiments completed its brief drill, Mr. Lincoln walked over and spoke with some of the ordinary soldiers. The president was tall, and he even towered over the Vermont boys in the Third. He was dreadfully thin as well, and his eyes betrayed his own lack of sleep and considerable anxiety. I exhaled with relief when he walked past me without noticing. Then he stopped, turned, and looked down from all his six-foot-plus height at me.

"Odd band," he remarked. "Just the one drummer."

"Just one drum," General Smith said, laughing. "You'll recall the story, sir."

"You don't look half the part," Mr. Lincoln said, touching my chin. "Your name is Willie, I understand."

"Y-y-y-yes, s-s-s-sir," I stammered.

"And how old are you?" the president asked.

"Twelve next month, sir," I said, trying to steady myself.

"Young to be a soldier," Mr. Lincoln said, growing pale. "Too young—"

"Look after yourself, son," General Franklin said, stepping between the president and me. The general guided Mr. Lincoln on down the line of regiments, leaving me standing there, a little bewildered.

When the regiments finished their parade, the other musicians and I were dismissed. We returned to the regiment to find that General Smith had ordered a special dinner for us. The general's own cook supervised the preparation, and the other young fortunates and I feasted on roasted pork, steamed carrots and potatoes, beans, and roasted ears of corn.

"You may have to do some more alterations," Julian jested when I rose to leave. "I believe you're larger now, Willie."

"Could be," I said, stretching myself. "I expect to sport chin whiskers any time."

"I wouldn't put any wager on that," Julian warned. "Of course, you can't exactly be in a rush, being only eleven."

"Guess not," I said, laughing. The chills returned then, and I shuddered.

"You all right?" Julian asked.

"Just tired," I told him. "Even Mr. Lincoln gets tired. Did you see how thin he was?"

"You probably reminded him of his own Willie," Julian told me. "That's his middle boy's name."

"Oh," I said, sighing. "I guess he was thinking how he wouldn't want his own boy out here."

"Only idiots and artists join this war at our age," he declared. "And I guess you know which of us is which."

I started to reply, but my legs buckled. I grew faint, and if Julian had not caught me, I would have collapsed.

"I better get you to your tent," he said, frowning. "You look done in."

"Am," I confessed. "My fingers are numb from drumming."

Julian helped me to my tent. Cal and Russ spread blankets over me, and I fell asleep fully dressed.

I awoke stiff, sore, and mightily confused. I was lying on a cot in Doc Jones's tent with a cool cloth on my forehead. "What?" I asked, fighting to focus my eyes. My head throbbed, and I tried to make sense of my surroundings. Someone had removed my uniform. I was dressed in an oversized nightshirt, and my bare toes protruded from under a cotton blanket.

"How are you feeling, Willie?" Dr. Jones asked. He

knelt at the side of the cot and squeezed my hand. Then he had a look at my tongue.

"None too good," I told him. "I suppose I ate too much."

"Nonsense," he growled. "Private Stebbins says you have been feverish since leaving Malvern Hill. Don't you know enough to fall out at sick call? I'm far too busy to go running from tent to tent, looking in on sick drummers."

"Sorry, Dr. Jones."

"You've got an intermittent fever, son," the doctor explained. "You won't be drumming for Company D for some time. I'm dispatching you on the next boat to Hampton. We have a good hospital there. They can take better care of you than I can."

"My pa—"

"I'll send for him, Willie," Dr. Jones promised. "He was worried when he heard. That Scott boy's been badgering me for a report as well. No visitors for a while, though. Rest first."

I closed my eyes and slept some more, but the doctor himself roused me a little later.

"Pa?" I asked.

"Later," Dr. Jones explained. "I would have kept everyone away another day, but my orders only hold so much weight. You have a special visitor, Willie."

I thought to ask, but I couldn't seem to get the words off my tongue. My curiosity was soon satisfied when General Smith stepped inside the tent.

"It appears we worked you a little too much," the general said, clasping my limp hand. "I'm sorry, Willie. No one told me you had a touch of fever."

"I'll get better," I assured him.

"I expect just that," he replied. "Half the army seems to be down with something, though. They're ordering some of the regiments back to Alexandria. I hope they will include my division. Meanwhile, it's to Hampton for you. Then Baltimore maybe."

"Yes, sir," I mumbled.

Later that afternoon Pa and Julian came in and sat with me. My head was a blur by then, though, and I was alternately freezing or boiling over with fever. I don't recall what I said, but Pa was concerned, and he kept asking Doc Jones if I would recover.

Julian and Dr. Jones located a brass bathtub somewhere, and they managed to heat water and maneuver my aching body into the contraption. I had never in my life had half so grand a bath. At home Ma poured a kettle of hot water into a wooden tub, and by the time my turn came, it was pretty tepid. Dirty, too. I thought how that tub came from the big house maybe. It was big enough that my skinny body slid right in, and I almost drowned.

The bath and some awful, bark-tasting medicine Doc Jones gave me restored some sense to me, but the fever and chills continued to take turns, and the following afternoon my tentmates carried me to the landing and put me aboard a supply steamer. By nightfall I was resting in the spotless Chesapeake General Hospital at Hampton, a short distance from Fort Monroe.

I had a reunion or two in that ward. Jace Wheeler was there, pale as death.

"You, too, eh?" he asked. Then he practically smiled. Some fellows are actually improved by sickness, I suppose.

Horace Partlow followed me to the hospital in July. Dr. Jones allowed Pa to visit on my birthday, and Pa brought a sketch Julian had made from memory of Mr. Lincoln and me.

Wheeler and Horace were both sent on north by ship, but I remained. The doctor worried the trip would make me worse, and I had to admit that weak as I was, I did not look forward to the rough seas that lay off the Virginia coast. It was hard staring out the big front window of the ward as steamers sailed past carrying the Army of the Potomac back to Alexandria. General McClellan's plan of taking the back door to Richmond had failed. The army was hurrying off north to protect Maryland from invasion.

12

I WAS STILL IN VIRGINIA that Christmas of 1862. While the Third Vermont bled on the snow-covered battleground at Fredericksburg, I tried to regain my strength. The chills and fever had lost their grip weeks earlier, but I had withered down to seventy pounds, and the doctors insisted I put some weight onto my bony limbs before departing the ward.

I never could stand to be left out of things, and those months in the hospital seemed to stretch into decades. I had been away from home last Christmas, but Pa had been with me. Now I had no one. The few fellows I met in the hospital never stayed long enough to become friends. Jace Wheeler visited on his way back to the regiment. He had deserted up North, but the provost caught up with him and sent him on to the Third.

I celebrated Christmas with the few soldiers left at the hospital. Most of them were victims of a measles outbreak at Fort Monroe, and the youngest was nineteen. I sang a few songs, but they wouldn't share a cake one of the freed slaves had baked for them, so I returned to my bed and passed the rest of the night alone. The next morning a letter arrived from Ma, which cheered me considerably. The doctors then ordered me down the hall, stripped me bare, and started up their poking and pinching again.

"He's still thin," one of them complained.

"What do you expect?" I asked. "The food's terrible here."

"Send him home," a bespectacled young surgeon declared. "He's right about the food. He needs home cooking more than he needs to stay around here."

In the end, they did not send me home. Instead, the first week of January I marched onto a schooner bound for Baltimore. I sailed north with seven other young soldiers in a single cabin, but I didn't mind. The walls kept most of the chill and all of the wind out, and the ship's cook brought us hot soup by the bucket. We ate until our bowls were empty, and then we filled them up again.

The ship docked two days later at Baltimore, and I was met by a tall, redheaded corporal.

"Johnston, Willie?" he called.

"That's me," I said, handing over a packet of papers.

"I'm Ben Sparks," he said, shaking my hand. "Don't let the stripes fool you, either. I'm just seventeen myself, and I'll thrash you if you try saluting or call me Corporal Sparks. I've never been more than Ben to anyone."

"Suits me, Ben," I said, grinning.

"They tell you anything?" he asked.

"No," I replied. "Only that I was going to Baltimore."

"You are assigned to the General Hospital, West's Building," he explained as he led me to a waiting ambulance.

"Not another hospital," I muttered.

"Oh, you're not a patient this time. The United States Army, in its wisdom, has decided all those months in the sick ward qualify you as a nurse."

"What?"

"That's right," Ben insisted. "You are now assigned to the hospital as a nurse."

My scowl must have said everything because Ben let me sit silently beside him on the ambulance seat as he nudged the solitary mule into a slow trot.

"It's not so bad," he assured me. He didn't seem to expect a reply, and I offered none. My year in the army had taught me that soldiers aren't really expected to enjoy themselves. Nor are they expected to think. Or complain. I'll admit that some don't think, but we nearly all complain.

Ben proved to be right about nursing duty, though. West's Building was just part of a large complex of hospital buildings, and the ward where I worked was full of soldiers recovering from wounds. There were young ones and old ones, and they were from every state left in the Union. I even saw a few from the Vermont Brigade, although none were from the Third. Best of all, I was paid eight months' wages, minus the cost of a uniform. It still came to almost ninety dollars. I kept five and mailed the rest home to Ma.

The doctors did most of the serious work at West's. After a time Ben taught me how to change a dressing, and I helped some of the men with their food. We had a little drummer, Terence Flynn, who was even shorter and skinnier than me. A rebel cannonball had taken Terry's right arm off, and I took over feeding him.

"I guess somebody will be doing this for me the rest of my life," he said sourly when I brought his dinner one day.

"No longer than you allow it," I told him. "You've still got a left hand. You may not be much good beating a drum, but you can feed yourself."

"How would you know?" he grumbled.

"Look here," I said, taking the spoon in my left hand and dipping it in the chicken broth. "Little children can feed themselves, and they fall over their own feet. I've seen men in here with both legs shot off who don't feel half as sorry for themselves as you do. If that ball had lopped off your head, sure, you could holler some. But an arm? That's nothing."

"You've got both of yours," he noted.

"Want me to cut mine off to make you feel better?"

He grinned for the first time when I took his knife and pointed it at my arm.

"That would be mighty stupid," he observed.

"I can't grow you another arm, Terry," I told him. "Nobody can. But I'll help you learn to use the left one. And until then, I'll loan you mine."

"It wouldn't fit," he said, "but I appreciate the offer. Anyway, you don't look well enough to spare it."

I did my best to puff myself up, but it was a failure. I told Terry about the months in the hospital, and he shared a frightful tale of how the Forty-second New York, his regiment, lost close to two hundred men at Antietam Creek back in September.

Every man in the hospital had his stories, and I listened to each one. Sometimes I wrote letters home for the ones with broken or amputated hands or arms. I did it for the blind men, too, and we had quite a few of them in West's Building. My penmanship was none too good, and my spelling was worse. Nobody seemed to mind, though. I offered to pen a letter for Terry, but he shook his head.

"I've only got an old aunt back home, and she wouldn't care," he explained. "I joined because my shoeshine customers all left to sign up. My pa always said I should follow the trade, you see."

By far the best days at West's were the rare occasions when visitors appeared. Sometimes a soldier's ma or sister would make the trip, and I never could decide which one was more welcome. We all saw our own mothers in those worried faces, and some of the men nearly came to blows over who got to talk to the sisters. In February we had a whole handful of girls from a female college. I volunteered to show them around, but for once Ben became Corporal Sparks. He escorted a pretty, freckle-faced eighteen-year-old from Annapolis from bed to bed while I did all the work!

Aside from feeding the wounded and writing letters, I took care of irksome duties like changing linen and cleaning up. Ben insisted on tending the bloodier wounds, and he always carted off the bodies when somebody died.

"I'm used to it," he said, turning me away. "Besides, you get so close to them."

He did, too, but I didn't argue. On February 12 Terry Flynn's stump festered, and the doctors carted him off to do some more cutting. They didn't bring him back.

"I think they knew it was hopeless," Ben told me afterward. "But with somebody so young, they needed to try."

"I suppose it didn't matter that he learned to use his left hand," I grumbled.

"I've seen a lot of men and more than a few boys pass through here," Ben said, sighing. "Lots die. I don't see many of them smile, and even fewer laugh. You made that little fellow happy a time or two, and that merits some pride on your part, Willie. Don't stop trying to help because you lose a man or two."

"Or a boy?"

"Exactly," Ben added. "I ever tell you why I stay here?"

"I never thought to ask, Ben."

"Most judge I don't care to rejoin my regiment."

"I wouldn't blame you," I explained. "Besides, you limp some."

"Yeah," Ben said, rolling up his trouser leg. I always thought there was flesh and bone down there, but I was wrong. Ben Sparks had a wooden leg.

"I never knew," I said, growing pale.

"Don't you tell anybody, Willie. I don't want their tears nor their sympathy. My regiment can't take me back, you see, and I won't go home and sip tea with the old ladies on my grandma's porch. I do some good here. You do, too."

"It hurts, though," I said, rubbing the moisture from my eyes. "When somebody like Terry up and dies."

"You start worrying when it doesn't," Ben advised. "When you get so hard and cold that you can look past the suffering, then you might as well be dead yourself. Everybody here deserves a tear or two, from us if from nobody else."

"I guess so," I agreed.

"You know so."

I never did get accustomed to patients' dying, and I tried to take everyone's minds off the sadness by sharing humorous episodes from the war. I read accounts of misadventures that were published in the newspapers, and I passed on others told to me by soldiers. Most of the men, especially the badly wounded ones, pleaded for news of the war. Ben or I would report on the campaigns after every meal. Things were looking better for the Union that spring, and we confidently predicted Richmond's fall.

One of the favorite stories enjoyed by all that March concerned a band of men sent south to spy on the rebels. They were led by a fellow named Andrews, and they wound up stealing a rebel train and tearing across the countryside. In the end, most were captured, and several were hanged, including Andrews himself. Six of the survivors became the first to receive a new medal granted by Congress.

"I wouldn't mind having one of those," a lanky New Yorker named Hendricks told me. "Only problem is that I never once did anything brave. I got myself shot running as fast as I could through a cornfield. If I had known the rebs were on both sides of us, I would have stayed put."

Personally, I didn't give much thought to medals. I had no girlfriend waiting for me back home, and Ma probably would make me stand up in church and show it off to the fat-faced old neighbor women. They liked to pinch my cheeks, and I couldn't abide that!

After I was in Baltimore eight months, Ben brought word that I was wanted at the hospital headquarters. I supposed that I was finally being sent back to the Third, but when I arrived, a tallish major decked out in yards of gold braid and wearing a gleaming sword took me aside.

"You're Willie Johnston, Third Vermont?" he asked.

"My father's also in the Third," I explained. "You might want him."

"He was also in Company D? A musician?"

"No, sir," I replied. "I suppose you have the right Johnston after all."

He led me down the hall to an orderly room. We

stepped inside together, and he drew a small notebook out of his pocket.

"Tell me about it," he suggested.

"About what?" I asked.

"Why, the Seven Days, of course."

By then the battles at Savage's Station and White Oak Swamp Bridge and Malvern Hill had been grouped together and called the Seven Days. I didn't care much for that notion, and I told the major that.

"Just describe what you saw, Willie," he instructed. "What you remember."

I did so. It didn't take long. So much had happened since then. I did recall the heat and the dust, and I remembered the sea of dead men at Malvern Hill. Most of all I remembered the day Mr. Lincoln came to Harrison's Landing.

"The president does make an impression, doesn't he?" the major asked.

"Yes, sir," I agreed.

The major left shortly thereafter, but he returned two days later.

"We have a short journey to make," he explained.

"I have my duties here," I pointed out.

"A replacement has been assigned. You have more important matters awaiting you."

"What matters?" I didn't like the sound of it one bit.

"I'll explain it all along the way. First, though, we need to get you ready."

Most days I wore an apron over my shirt and ignored my tunic altogether. Tending the wounded, you were apt to get blood on your clothes. We sent the aprons to the laundry every night and took a fresh one. That way we kept a good deal cleaner.

Now the major escorted me to the bathing room. Somehow he had assembled a brand-new uniform for me. Boots, too. I gazed in wonder at a real leather belt and spotless white leggings. A cap with a brass bugle in front lay atop a new tunic.

"Get scrubbed," the major ordered, pointing to a waiting tub of steaming hot water. "I'll send a man in to clip your hair. See he shaves you as well."

"Shaves me?" I asked, tensing.

"You've got a whisker or two on your chin. That won't do."

He left, and I shed my clothes. Then I climbed in the tub, soaped myself, and rinsed properly. I can't recall ever feeling so absolutely clean. I was halfway dressed when a young black man arrived. He insisted I sit on a stool and remain absolutely rigid.

"You the barber?" I asked.

"That's what they tell me," he said. "Mostly I clip hair for the undertakers. It's a real art, making the dead presentable."

"I'm not dead," I reminded him.

"No, but by the time you get all prettied up, you'll look good enough to bury. Don't you worry. I shave myself every morning, and I haven't cut my throat yet."

"I just have a whisker or two," I told him.

"You leave everything to me, youngster. A man's first shave ought to be a first-class job. I'll do you justice."

He mixed some shaving powder and hot water in his hands. Then he spread the lather across my chin and cheeks. He put an edge of the razor to my face and sliced away my chin hairs so quickly I hardly had time to notice. He then took out scissors and trimmed my hair. When he finished, I looked ready for Easter Sunday.

He left, and I continued dressing. I took great pains to make sure every button was fastened. I was reaching for the cap when the major reappeared.

"Now that's what I call a soldier," he declared.

"I'm only a drummer," I explained. "Lately not even that."

"I know all about you, Johnston," the major insisted. "Follow me. We have a train to catch."

We rode to the station in grand style. The major had hired a cab, and we traveled the streets of Baltimore like a pair of princes. The major flashed a pass at the depot, and we were admitted to the First Class Car. A waiter served us platters of roast beef and boiled potatoes, and I stuffed myself. I had to pass up a slice of chocolate cake for fear my trousers would split.

I paid only scant attention to the countryside outside the window, but when we stopped, I recognized Washington right away. The major and I stepped off the train in the center of town, not far from the Capitol itself. It looked grand with its new dome, but I had little time to observe architecture. Once again the major ordered a cab. The driver smiled at me as he poked his horse into a gallop. We raced along the dusty streets, and I worried that if the cab's wheel hit a rock, all my efforts to improve my appearance would have been for naught. Fortunately we arrived without incident outside the War Department building.

"I don't understand any of this," I said, refusing to climb the steps. "What am I doing here?"

"You are seeing Secretary Stanton," the major said, pulling me along. "He has something for you."

As bewildered as ever, I stumbled up the steps and followed the major to a small room outside a larger reception room. I could see a handful of generals and finely dressed ladies inside. There were several distinguished men in tailored suits, too. I also recognized one of the war correspondents who had visited our camp in Virginia.

"Wait there, Willie," the major said, pointing to a small sofa. I stepped over and sat down. I let out a long breath and shook my head. Then I felt a strong hand grasp my shoulder.

"Hello, son," a faintly familiar voice called.

I stiffened my shoulders and gazed up at Mr. Lincoln himself. He wore a friendly grin this time, and his eyes were not so tired as before.

"Good afternoon, sir," I said, starting to rise.

"No need, Willie," he told me. "Mind if I join you here?"

"I'd be honored," I told him.

"You seem to have lost your stammer," he observed. "That's for the best. I had one myself a long time back, but I was determined to be a lawyer. Works against a man, stammering."

"Yes, sir," I agreed. "I was a little nervous before."

"Tired as well. Quite a thing, holding on to your drum during that long withdrawal."

"More a skedaddle than a withdrawal," I observed.

"General McClellan wouldn't agree. He's after my job, you know."

"I imagine you will hold on to it, sir. You look the part."

"My own Willie told me that once."

"Trust us to know, sir."

"He's left me now," Mr. Lincoln said, frowning. "We buried him better than a year ago now."

"Was he a soldier then?" I asked.

"No, just a little boy. I wouldn't allow him to join the army. He had the heart for it, but his health . . . He died of a fever here in Washington."

"We've had a bad time with fevers in the army. I had a battle with one myself."

"You have had your share of challenges, Willie. General Smith spoke well of you, and Secretary Stanton agrees that you exemplify the spirit of all our soldiers. You have served your country well, and the nation has decided to honor you."

"Honor me?" I asked. "How?"

"Why don't we go see?" the president suggested. "I think they are ready in there."

I spied the major and rose when he waved me along. I entered the room with my cap on, and the major motioned for me to remove it. I did so, and one of the ladies grinned. The generals didn't. The onlookers formed an aisle, and I marched past them to where a large man with a peculiar stripe of gray in his hair waited. He read a short statement about the Seven Days and told how I kept my drum when all the other drummers in General Smith's division failed to do so. He spoke a few words about my time in the hospital and congratulated me on my recovery.

"By virtue of the authority granted by the United States Congress, I now award Drummer Willie Johnston of the Third Vermont Volunteers the Congressional Medal of Honor."

"Shake Secretary Stanton's hand," the major whispered.

I almost fainted. The secretary of war himself clasped my hand. He then pinned a strip of ribbon holding a star-shaped pendant onto my tunic.

"May all our citizens demonstrate the devotion shown by this young man," the secretary added. The generals applauded, and the ladies came forward to kiss my forehead and pinch my cheek. It was every bit as bad as if Ma had invited the neighbor ladies.

Later, I tried to stand as tall and stiff as possible while a newspaper artist made a sketch. The correspondents fired a volley of questions, but I hardly heard them. I was glancing around, hoping the president would reappear.

"Has anyone seen Mr. Lincoln?" I finally asked.

"He has a country to run," one of the generals observed. "You shouldn't expect him to be here. I don't believe you're quite that important, son."

I thought about telling him about the visit before the ceremony, but I knew better than to antagonize a general. I kept mum. Only when the major had us on the northbound train that night did I ask anyone about anything.

"Why me?" I asked, fingering the medal. "I did nothing very brave. I never stole a rebel locomotive."

"I don't know for certain, Willie," the major replied. "Maybe it had something to do with the president's son. You certainly touched his heart. I like to think that when the secretary pinned the medal on you today he was honoring all the sons of all the fathers who have served the nation in this terrible ordeal. We can't recognize everyone, so we chose you as their representative. You should consider yourself very special, Willie."

"I do, sir, but I don't feel like I have a right to."

"I probably don't have a right to wear a major's uniform, Willie. I haven't led any charges or braved any bullets. I think a man has to serve where and how his country asks, though. I do. And so will you."

"And if my name had been Terry or Ben?"

"Somebody else might have received the medal. But then Ben didn't carry his drum to Harrison's Landing, either, did he?"

"No, sir," I admitted.

"You have a lot of years left to you, Willie. When you're older, you may come to understand how important it is for a country to have heroes, to honor courage and devotion. If we can't see those good things in the midst of so much death and suffering, we may be unable to continue this fight. I believe in courage and devotion, and I have witnessed both at West's. Glance around at the men's faces when you walk among them with that medal on your chest. If they tell you to send it back, do so. They won't, though."

It was a strange thing. Aside from Pa and a few of my teachers, no grown man had ever spoken so many words aimed directly at my heart. I never even knew his name, either. He was right about the men at the hospital, too.

"It's about time they recognized a real soldier," one of them declared. "You make us all proud, Willie."

I didn't reply. Among the brotherhood of soldiers, some things were simply understood. I paraded through the ward one final time. Then I stripped off my tunic, draped an apron over my shirt, and went back to work.

Epilogue

WHEN WILLIE JOHNSTON RECEIVED THE CONGRESSIONAL Medal of Honor on September 16, 1863, he became the seventh soldier in the U.S. Army to be so honored. He remains the youngest ever to qualify for this nation's highest military decoration, being not quite twelve when distinguishing himself during the Seven Days.

Willie remained at the U.S. General Hospital in Baltimore through January 1864 as a member of what was first called the Invalid Corps and later more appropriately renamed the Veteran Volunteers. At that time he completed his three-year enlistment and was mustered out of the army. He then reenlisted in the Third Vermont, was allowed a brief visit home to see his mother, and reported for duty with his old regiment in Virginia. He ended up serving the remainder of the war with the regimental brass band in Baltimore.

Although some of the characters in this book are fictional, they represent the courage and self-sacrifice of all Civil War soldiers, Northern and Southern alike. The soldiers of Company D, Third Vermont Infantry, portrayed in this novel are the actual men who lived and died in the dramatic struggle to preserve the Union and abolish slavery. I have relied on the compiled service records preserved in the U.S. National Archives, the records of the U.S. Census of 1860, and the *Revised Roster of Vermont Volunteers of the Civil War* (Watchman Publishing Co., 1892) for details.

Captain Fernando Harrington was discharged from the army on July 23, 1862, under mysterious circumstances. Although his official report of the skirmish at Lee's Mills survives as the accepted account of the Third Vermont's role in that fight, later versions provided by veteran soldiers after the war claim the captain remained well to the rear. Captain Sam Pingree was acknowledged as the hero of the hour.

Erastus Buck eventually rose to the rank of captain. He died May 22, 1864, from wounds received leading Company I. He left behind letters recently published in *Buck's Book: A View of the 3rd Vermont Infantry Regiment* (edited by John E. Balzer, Balzer & Associates, 1993). The account serves as an important source of information on the regiment and its men.

Fifer artist Julian Scott himself received the Medal of Honor in recognition of his gallantry in rescuing wounded comrades at Lee's Mills. His sketches attracted great interest, and he was discharged from the army and sent to art school. Before the war ended, Julian returned as a correspondent. His sketches and paintings of soldiers and war reflect an appreciation for the drama as well as the humor of army life. One painting in particular, a depiction of drummer boys playing cards on a makeshift table, provides a glimpse of the army's youngest soldiers.

Sergeant Bill Currier later won promotion to first lieutenant. He survived the war. Horace Partlow's illness led to his discharge on November 14, 1862. Moses Torrence was likewise discharged due to illness, in October 1862. Silome Persons was captured at Savage's Station and later exchanged. In May 1864 he was wounded, but he recovered and returned home. Calvin Stebbins left the Third Vermont in October 1862 to join the cavalry. Calvin Stevens continued to suffer from sickness, but eventually won promotion to corporal. His younger brother, Russell, was killed in the Third Vermont's attack on Fort Stevens on July 12, 1864.

The memory of Will Scott, the "sleeping sentinel," is preserved by a monument erected near his home in Groton, Vermont. He is better remembered for his minor lapse on picket duty than for his sacrifice at Lee's Mills.

Acknowledgments

THE SEARCH FOR WILLIE JOHNSTON proved long and often difficult. In addition to his father, there was also another soldier in the Third Vermont named William Johnson. Even today the records of the three soldiers are intermingled. It required a personal visit to the National Archives in Washington, D.C., to unravel all the particulars. I am grateful to the research staff for their many kindnesses and great help as I pored through the more than one thousand service records of the soldiers who served in the Third Vermont. The regional archives center in Fort Worth provided me with census records and suggestions for acquiring microfilm copies of the Third Vermont's monthly returns, the best account of where and when the regiment served.

As always when I am searching for reference books and materials on the Civil War, I received great help from the Confederate Research Center at Hill County College in Hillsboro, Texas. They let you read about Yankees there, too, and their library of rare texts is superb. The librarians of the Plano Public Library aided in securing books through that great aid to research, the interlibrary loan program.

Finally, I have always found a book comes to life for me when I walk the battlefields and touch the ground. The personnel at the Richmond National Battlefield Park and the Fort Monroe Casement Museum aided my search for the often elusive sites where the Third Vermont camped, fought, and died. I am grateful to these fine people for taking a few extra minutes from their taxing schedule to improve my understanding of the Peninsular Campaign.

—G. Clifton Wisler
Plano, Texas

About the Author

G. CLIFTON WISLER, the author of more than fifty-five books for children and adults, has received numerous honors for his writing. One of his most recent books for young adults, *Red Cap,* was named an American Library Association Best Book for Young Adults and a Child Study Association Book of the Year.

An avid American history buff, Mr. Wisler lives in Plano, Texas.